She Smells the Dead

Also by E.J. Stevens

From the Shadows
Shadows of Myth and Legend

She Smells the Dead

ଽ୬ଔ

E.J. Stevens

Sacred Oaks Press
ৼৡ

Published by Sacred Oaks Press
Sacred Oaks, 221 Sacred Oaks Lane, Wells, Maine 04090

First Printing (trade paperback edition), August 2010

Stevens, E.J.
She Smells the Dead / E.J. Stevens

ISBN 978-0-9842475-2-3 (trade pbk.)

Printed in the United States of America

PUBLISHER'S NOTE
This is a work of fiction. Names, characters, places, and
incidents either are the product of the author's imagination
or are used fictitiously, and any resemblance to actual
persons, living or dead, business establishments, events, or
locales is entirely coincidental.

For my family and friends

Thank you for always believing
& helping me find true magic in my life

Prologue

I can smell the dead. I know, you hear of people with superhuman paranormal powers and you think, *how cool is that* but there is nothing cool about smelling the dead. I mean it could be worse I suppose. The dead don't smell like rotting corpses, usually. It's often more of a symbolic smell. "Smell Impressions" as my friend Calvin likes to call them. Ugh. I know, again with the uncoolness. You have *no* idea.

Imagine biting into your favorite veggie burger loaded up with ketchup and suddenly smelling rotten eggs. Heck, my biggest fear is finally kissing Garrett Hamlin, the guy I've been drooling over since 8th grade, and smelling something awful. Like skunk butt or sweaty gym socks. I. Would. Die.

So yah. My name is Vanessa Stennings but I go by Yuki. When you're a kid the name Nessie gets you teased and Vee for victory takes on a whole new meaning when you reach high school and all the boys can think about is getting lucky. So I picked Yuki. It means *snow* or a *snow covered village* which, considering all the snow we get here in Maine, seems fitting. I didn't pick it for that reason though. I decided on Yuki because the smell of freshly falling snow is a clean, beautiful smell and if I'm anything, it's ruled by smells.

Of course I hadn't realized that a few jocks would start calling me Yucky, but heck, they're *jocks*. It's not like I acknowledge their existence anyway. We live in different

worlds. They are obsessed with muscles and fart jokes--
and I smell the dead.

Chapter 1

I was staring at my black nail polish which was now chewed around the edges and wondering if I now had black flecks in my teeth. *Great.* It was only second period of the first day of school and I was already a nervous wreck. How was I ever going to survive an entire school year when I couldn't even make it through one day?

Vinegar. Strong, pungent apple cider vinegar. It made my mouth water and my eyes burn. The smell also made me think of dyeing Easter eggs as a kid. Funny how smell could take you back inside a memory. But this wasn't a real smell, unless one of my classmates was wearing eau du pickles; it was a smell impression.

I was sitting in second period English class and I was smelling dead people. *Groovy.* Maybe I was being haunted by the Ghost of Easter Past. *Let's not go there.* The Easter Bunny always did creep me out with his gigantic teeth and wide-eyed permagrin. *Yah Yuki, let's not go there.*

Trying my best to take notes while my eyes were watering would at least keep my mind off Mr. Pickle Pants. There wasn't much I could do for him until I got out of school for the day. The smelly dead dude would just have to wait.

Chapter 2

I had changed into comfy yoga pants and my favorite hoodie and was now ready to tackle the mystery of my new smelly friend. I grabbed my laptop, notebook, and pen and plumped my nest of pillows up at the top of my bed. *I might as well make myself comfortable.* I had learned over summer vacation that these hauntings would stop when I figured out what the ghost wanted. The problem was that all I had to go on was a smell impression and it's not like I had a fancy CSI lab for analyzing clues. I had one clue, a strong vinegar smell, and no idea where to begin. I was probably going to be smelling vinegar for the rest of my life. *Might as well get on with it.*

My research methods were extremely advanced. I Googled vinegar. I then tried limiting the search parameters to include Maine and exclude recipes. Amazing detective work I know. I scrolled through page after page until I felt like my eyes were bleeding. I was about to close the search window when a link caught my attention. It was to an obituary in Maine that included the word vinegar. *Indubitably.*

My heart started racing and I suddenly felt dizzy. I probably shouldn't have skipped both lunch and dinner, but you try eating when everything smells like vinegar. If this lead panned out I might be able to eat a late night snack and if not, then I would just have to stop and grab some salt and vinegar chips on the way to school tomorrow. With a plan in place I tried to refocus on the computer screen.

Obituaries

Jackson Green, 81 was laid to rest today in
Pine Hill cemetery outside Sansborough
Maine. Jackson is survived by his wife Grace.
He was predeceased by his three sons,
Richard Green, Jonathan Green, and Samuel
Green, who passed away in a tragic boating
accident this past June. Jackson Green was
CEO of the Green Orchards Apple Cider
Vinegar Company. His fortune was to be left
to his wife Grace Green, however, his last will
and testament seems to have been misplaced
some time just before his death. Anyone with
information regarding the whereabouts of Mr.
Green's Will is asked to please contact the
local Sansborough police department.

I jumped as I heard a knock and my bedroom door
opened. *Maybe I was just a little jittery.*

Calvin stood there leaning against the doorway with
his thumbs in his jean pockets and his shaggy brown hair
hanging in his eyes. "Hey Yuki. You seemed kind of
down at school today. Thought I'd stop by to cheer you
up," he said with a wry grin. "Your mom let me in."

Of course she did. My mom loved Calvin.

For a second I was glad that I had changed into my
hoodie and yoga pants and not into my girlie pajamas
when I realized I was worried about what I looked like in
front of *Calvin.* This haunting really did have me messed
up. I started to smile nonchalantly as Cal walked in and
tossed his backpack on my bed. It was then that I saw
what he was pulling out of it. Oh no, not another dung
beetle plushie. He was never going to let me live this
down. *Ever.*

"Thought this might cheer you up," he said as he set it
atop my laptop.

You suck Calvin Miller. You suck times ten. The beetle plushie was an inside joke and a way to tease me that Calvin never tired of.

Calvin was very Zen and into all things mystical. Heck, maybe that was why he was always following me around. A few years back he decided we should go to a Shamanism retreat and discover our spirit animals. At first I dismissed the idea as one of Calvin's hokey hair brained ideas. Right up until he called me shallow and incapable of spiritual awakening or some other mumbo jumbo. So yah, I went to Shaman Camp.

Calvin was in hippie Heaven and I was, of course, in total Hell. It was muddy and buggy and everyone wanted to hold hands and be one with each other, or mother earth, or *something*. I just wanted to crawl inside myself and disappear. He got to sit there cross-legged in his cargo shorts and hemp necklace looking all tanned and buff and *dirty* while I was sweating in my layers of black skirts, tights, and long sleeve tee. At least I had my 14-eye boots on. There was mud *everywhere*.

My plan was to stick around until the animal totem workshop ceremony thing was over and then find a way home, *fast*. I was supposed to lay in the mud and journey on my spirit animal, or power animal as some of the guys were calling it, but since I refused I ended up picking drying mud off my Doc Martens while the head shaman dude had a vision and declared my spirit animal to be a beetle. *What?* He went on about the beetle representing resurrection. Something about how in ancient Egypt the scarab beetle would form a piece of ox dung into a ball, then fill it with eggs, and roll it from East to West. *Uhm hello, gross?* The beetle would then wait a month and dig up her ball of kiddoes and toss it into water where the little beetle babes would hatch. Beetles tossing egg filled poo into water in Egypt? This couldn't be *my* spirit animal, right? *Or maybe I was just in de-Nile.*

So ever since Shaman Camp Calvin would bring up my fab spirit animal as the dung beetle and I would remind him it was the sacred scarab, though if I were honest with myself even that sounded lame. What kind of universe would shackle me with such a crappy (o.k. go ahead and laugh) spirit animal? What made the whole situation even worse were the spirit animals that everyone else got. The girl named Sky received an eagle, some guy with dreads a tiger, a red haired girl ended up with a fox, and Calvin a wolf. Of course Calvin would receive something über cool like a wolf, but did I have to end up with a dung beetle? It just wasn't fair.

So I glared at the beetle plushie and grumbled, "sacred scarab" at the same moment Calvin said, "dung beetle."

I sighed, rolling my eyes to my bedroom ceiling, and asked, "I'm never going to win this one am I?"

"Nope. Never," he replied, so quickly I knew he had been waiting for the question. "So you tuned into your Smellavision?" he asked casually.

Was he worried about me? *Nah*. Calvin just liked to goad me and he knew how much my newfound paranormal power bothered me. "Oh yah, in full Technosmellor," I quipped, only to inwardly groan. *Technosmellor*? What was up with me today? There was something seriously wrong with my head.

"If you don't help me before I have to skip another meal, *I'll* be the ghost and I'll come back to haunt *you*," I said with one hand on my hip and the other pointing at his chest.

Calvin leaned in inches from my face, with my finger now pressing against his chest, wearing a lazy grin. "I could only wish for that kind of haunting. You smell like strawberries Yuki. Who wouldn't want to be haunted by you?"

His eyes were so blue. *Wait, what*? Was he teasing me or was he serious? Then with those gorgeous blue eyes, *had they always been that shade of blue*, he winked at me and pulled away. What the heck did that mean? Was Calvin Miller *flirting* with me? No way. He was just a friend, an *annoying* friend who liked to tease me. That's all it was. Cal was just teasing me. No big. *Right*.

"It doesn't work like that," I claimed. At least I didn't think it did. God, I was such a mess! I couldn't think straight. I jumped up off the bed and starting pacing my bedroom floor. I just needed to stretch my legs, right? *Sure*. "This is what I have so far," I said pushing my laptop towards him and accidentally knocking the beetle plushie to the floor behind the bed. "It's a weird coincidence, isn't it?" I asked as I resumed my pacing. "This vinegar smell impression and a dead guy with some big vinegar empire inheritance scandal?" O.k. I was probably exaggerating a bit, but the pieces did all seem to fall together. Peeking at Calvin out of the corner of my eye I nearly tripped over my own feet. *Slick Yuki, real slick*. Fortunately he seemed too focused on reading the obituary to notice.

"Yuki, you have plans after school tomorrow?" Calvin turned to me and asked.

How does he raise one brow like that? Does he practice in the mirror?

"Nope, no plans yet," I said flipping my hair as I looked at him over my shoulder. *I can use cool poses too Calvin Miller*.

"Good we can take my truck and head out to this farm after school," he said as he stood up and stretched showing a bit of tanned washboard abs.

Not that I was looking.

"I'll check the online maps when I get home and sketch out some directions. Don't forget to eat. You're looking even more pale than usual," he said as he grabbed his backpack and sauntered out the door.

At a loss for what to say, I nearly thanked him for the beetle plushie. *I was so not doing that.* "Uhm, sure. See you tomorrow," I said to his receding back. *Son of a dung beetle.* He had made me feel like an idiot, *again*.

Chapter 3

*S*enior year day two. *Only a gazillion more days to go.*

"Witch," Jay Freeman sniped at me as he pushed past me in the hall, nearly dumping the contents of my backpack. He said it like he was spitting out something foul tasting.

Whatever.

Some of the J-team jocks and cheerleader bimbettes started calling me that Freshman year. It was lame then and it was beyond lame now. *If they only knew.* I had never practiced witchcraft, though what I knew of Wicca and herb lore from Calvin was pretty cool, but try explaining that to the J-team.

Freshman year I bought this silver evil eye pendant. Calvin was with me at the time, shopping in this little import store in Portland, and he said it was for good luck. I thought it looked kind of creepy with my all black ensemble, so I bought it and put it on right there in the store. *Plus, who couldn't use some good luck?*

I was still wearing it when Jared Zempter fell on his face in front of me while playing basketball in gym class. I've always been uncomfortable in the gym. It was like a pedestal for jocks to strut their stuff. *Gag me.* So I was fidgeting with my necklace while sitting on the bench wearing my faded Depeche Mode t-shirt and ripped skull tights. I wasn't even paying attention to the class, which just made the situation worse. Jared and his friends claimed that I was in a trance, how embarrassing, and using my evil eye pendant to channel my dark powers. *Great.*

By the time I changed out of my gym clothes and ran to the cafeteria for lunch, the J-team had spread rumors to the entire school.

"So Yuki, I hear you killed a cat for a blood sacrifice and called upon the powers of Satan to make Jared Zempter trip in gym class," Calvin said as I set my lunch tray on the table.

"Yah, it couldn't possibly have had anything to do with his sneaker laces being untied," I grumbled. I pushed food around on my plate making little food sculptures wondering if anyone would even remember all this by the next day. *Apparently they had.*

Could this day get much worse? Wait. I should never tempt fate by asking that question. Things can always get worse. I must have lousy karma. What could I have been in my last life that would cause such horrible luck for me now? *Probably a dung beetle.* I started to laugh, but then realized I didn't need to give the J-team more fodder for making fun of me. With my luck they'd snap a picture of me laughing to myself in the hall and it would end up in the school paper. I can see the headline now, "Evil Witch Yuki laughs maniacally while communing with her spirit minions." I guess it wouldn't be that far from the truth. I may not be able to speak to spirits *but I could smell the dead.*

"Hey! Yuki-sama," Gordan Avery said as he ran up to me. Gordy was in the anime club with me and thought I was some kind of hero for changing my name to Yuki.

"Cal gave me another dung beetle plushie last night," I said gravely.

"Want me to take him out for you?" Gordy asked in his hit-man gruff voice.

"Nah, I was thinking of bringing him to anime club next week though," I said and laughed. I couldn't keep a straight face for long while talking to Gordy.

"Oh o.k., I'll make sure to queue up some yaoi. Loveless made him squirm last time you were mad at him," Gordy said laughingly.

"Ah Gordy, you're the best. Thanks! See you there." I had to run to get to physics class before the bell rang.

Chapter 4

I stared at the clock as it tick-ticked its way through the last period of the day. When the last bell rang I already had my bag slung over my shoulder and was half-way up the row of desks. The vinegar smell was getting worse and I couldn't wait to get on the road with Calvin and solve the case of Mr. Smelly so I could be back to normal life. It had nothing to do with seeing Calvin. *Nothing at all.*

He was waiting for me by his truck with his head tilted up like he was sunning himself.

"Hey skin cancer! You ready to go?" I shouted over at him. I had hoped to startle him and break his calm, cool façade but he just slowly opened his eyes and stretched.

"Sure Dung Beetle Princess, ready when you are," he said as he jingled his keys.

Oh boy, this was going to be a pleasure trip. I just rolled my eyes and jumped up on the running board so I could climb up into the passenger seat. "Ew, it smells like wet dog in here," I complained.

Calvin just swung up into the driver seat and grinned his toothy smile at me. "Well my spirit animal *is* a wolf," he said as he started the engine and backed the truck out of the parking space. "It could be worse. It could smell like your spirit animal Yuki," he said and coughed a little to cover his chuckle.

Oh yah, laugh it up big guy.

"Well, it smells gross. You should think about hosing it out or something," I said while wondering why it smelled like wet dog in here when I knew Calvin's family didn't have any pets.

He just shrugged and waited for the traffic light to change and then turned his truck, *his smelly truck*, onto the highway that would take us close to the Green family farm. He was doing me a favor driving me out to the farm, so I tried not to complain anymore about his truck hygiene. But just for the record? *Wet dog and vinegar just don't mix.*

Just when I thought I wouldn't be able to take the sensory overload we turned onto a gravel drive and Calvin pulled to the side of the road. I rolled down the window to try to catch my breath and settle my stomach. The wet dog smell did seem to fade a little, but the vinegar smell just became stronger. "I guess this is the place," I said wincing at the headache beginning in my temples. Now that we were here I had no idea what to do next. *It's not like I had time to come up with a plan or anything.*

Calvin, however, must have spent the entire school day scheming. "O.k. you're name is Cindy and you're doing a school report on organic farms in the area," he said, "I learned on the Internet that the Green family was clever and when organic farming became popular they played on their name and became a 'green' farm."

So apparently he had worked on this plan through the night as well. *Yup, I'm a slacker. Thanks Calvin Miller for making me look bad.*

I grabbed a notebook and pen from my school bag preparing for the part I was about to play. *Stalling for time.* I'm not good at acting. In school I leave the drama to the cheerleader bimbettes. If I were really honest with myself I'd have to admit that I was scared. How was I going to lie to a grieving widow and figure out what this ghost needed so he could move on?

"Can I just use my real name?" I asked Calvin, "I'm not good at lying. I think I'll do a better job if I only have to exaggerate the truth about the school report."

He looked at me a bit weird, maybe a little disappointed, but then shrugged, "Sure. Yuki it is then." and pulled back out onto the gravel road.

We didn't have far to go, but Cal drove slowly, giving us a chance to scope out the place. It was a gorgeous farm. I was no expert, but there were apple orchards on one side of the road and rows of grape vines on the other. At the top of the hill there was an old farmhouse and in the opposite field were a tower of white boxes I recognized as bee hives. I laughed at the thought of my friend Emma's mortification at what she called "bee oppression."

Emma and I had discussed bee oppression last semester after I had used a different shoe polish on my boots. She had run up admiring my boots and asked what color polish I had used.

"Oxblood," I replied, immediately wishing I could take it back.

Emma blanched. Emma had pale skin and long pale blond hair so when she went an even lighter shade of pale she nearly disappeared against the ivory wall behind her.

"Um, there's no real blood in it though," I said lamely hoping she wasn't going to cry or throw up.

Emma was really sensitive, especially when it came to animal cruelty. I was vegetarian but Emma was vegan. I waited for the tears, but instead she started to laugh. It started as a nervous giggle, but grew so that we were nearly falling over with laughter when Cal walked by. He did that eyebrow thing of his and we just started laughing harder. He kept walking by, but I could have sworn his shoulders were shaking as he turned the corner down the hall.

"Oh Yuki, I'm more grossed out by the cow that had to die for those boots," she sighed wiping tears from her eyes.

That was when she had told me about bee oppression and how as a vegan she didn't eat honey. It was actually kind of interesting and after her calling it bee puke for over an hour I couldn't eat honey either.

Coming back to the current situation I thought dreamily that maybe I could get a school paper out of this gig after all. Apparently the Green Farm used bee slave labor to pollinate their crops. I'm sure Emma would help me write an outraged paper on the topic.

"Hey freak, what are *you* doing here?" a disgusted voice griped behind me.

I nearly jumped out of my skin. I turned around and realized I must have died and been sent straight to Hell because standing there in front of me was Jared Zempter, the devil himself, holding a pitchfork. I had to bite my lip to keep from laughing at him.

Jared was wearing tall rubber boots with muddy jeans and I realized belatedly, I know the pitchfork should have clued me in, that he must be working here at the farm. *Just my luck.* Normally a kid from my school working here would have been a break for me. *Yah, if he were human.* Instead this was rapidly turning into a major disaster.

"Bee oppression," I said hoping to throw him off guard. *Where the heck was Cal?* I could really use some backup. The smell of vinegar was getting so strong I felt like I was going to pass out. *Patience Ghost Dude, I'm working on it.*

"Hey Jared, maybe you could help me," Calvin said with a fake grin on his face.

We had been friends since second grade, I could tell when he was faking his outward passivity. Jared just looked back and forth from me to Calvin with a bewildered look on his face. *Jocks and bullies are not known for their high intelligence.*

"Hey man," Calvin said trying to draw Jared's attention, "I heard they might be hiring here now that old man Green is gone. Yuki just came along for the ride," he said somewhat dismissively turning attention away from me.

They started talking somewhat civilly about jobs and farm stuff and I tried to concentrate on my smell impression. *Come on Spidey sense don't fail me now.*

I slowly turned 360 degrees while trying to look like I was just bored and taking in the scenery. The vinegar smell was strongest when I faced the house on the hill and what I realized was probably a barn out behind it. Sighing inwardly I started walking casually up the hill. I stopped a few times to admire things growing on the ground.

When it became apparent that Jared was too busy talking to Calvin to pay attention to the freak, *moi*, I hustled up to the front of the house. It was a typical white colonial farmhouse, though in better shape than most I had seen. The paint wasn't peeling and the porch wasn't sagging. I wondered again at how this family could lose the inheritance that Mr. Green was said to have left behind. They obviously had, or recently had possessed, a fair amount of money. It would take a large amount of money to keep the farm going and the buildings and road in such good repair. Even the fencing around the orchards and vineyards looked to be picture perfect. *So what is wrong with this picture?*

I caught a whiff of wet dog just as I sensed someone behind me. I turned as Calvin reached for my hand.

"Come on Yuki, let's head back to the truck," Calvin said as he led me back down the hill.

I guess that was all the reconnaissance we were going to manage for today. *Sorry Mr. Green. We'll try again tomorrow.* On the ride back I tried to laugh along with Calvin about Jared and the J-team, but I couldn't help but feel a bit depressed. I wanted to help the ghost of Jackson Green find peace. I also wanted to stop smelling vinegar. *It was giving me a headache.*

Chapter 5

I sat in third period daydreaming about Garrett Hamlin asking me to the homecoming dance. I wasn't usually into those things but this was senior year and I heard that Garrett and his girlfriend Nadine had broken up over summer break. *Yes.* Now I just had to turn on the Yuki charm and get Garrett to ask me to the dance. That would give me an excuse to wear the black corset dress I found in Salem last winter. I bought it after the Halloween rush when most of the shops were closing for a few months. It had been hanging in my closet just waiting for a chance to be worn. That chance was coming. *I could feel it.*

Or maybe it was just the non-stop vinegar smell going to my head. *This has to stop or I am going to go insane.* I tried to make it through the remainder of class thinking about Garrett. He was totally my type. He dressed all in black, with the big chunky boots that made him absolutely tower over me, not that he needed them. Garrett was 6'1" without the boots and I was 5' nothing even when I piled all my hair on top of my head. He was perfection wrapped in a pretty, bad boy package. Garret always wore black eyeliner that made his emerald green eyes pop. He had dead straight dyed black hair in an asymmetrical cut that usually hid his right eye giving him a mysterious look. It also showed off the row of silver studs running up and down his ear. *Yum.*

Calvin always scoffed that Garrett used so much hair gel to hold his hair in place that he ended up with helmet head. *Right.* What did Calvin know? He always looked like a shaggy dog that just shook his head and let it dry.

What was Calvin doing interrupting my Garrett daydream anyway? *Why was I thinking about Cal?*

It had to be the smell bombardment. It was throwing me off my game. With a sigh and silent prayer for some higher power to give me strength I focused back on the mystery of Jackson Green and his missing inheritance. I was convinced the missing money had something to do with why he was still connected to this plain of existence. The boating accident that killed his three sons also seemed suspicious. *Oh emm gees.* What if Jackson Green didn't die of old age? *What if Jackson Green was murdered?*

I don't know why I hadn't thought of it before. I guess I just saw his advanced age and that idyllic farm and thought he must have passed away peacefully. Well, except for the part about him haunting me, but I figured he was going to lead me to the missing money which I could help deliver to his widow and voila, no more vinegar smell. I never considered that his spirit might lead me to a murderer. I was going to hope for the best, but prepare for the worst. I wasn't going anywhere near that farm without backup. I was going to have to ask Calvin for a favor. *Wonderful.*

This was probably going to cost me. Maybe I could treat Cal to his favorite Indian restaurant. Nothing a little Tandoori can't fix, right? I tried sneaking a text to him before the end of school, "Wanna grab curry l8er? My treat." and hit send before I could chicken out. It was just dinner with Cal right? No big. So why were my hands shaking so bad I could hardly send the text? Just as the final bell rang my phone vibrated. I looked down to see Calvin's text, "sure, pick u up at 7?" "Sure," I lamely texted back. For some reason I felt sick as I grabbed my bag and walked out of class. *Son of a dung beetle.* I was nervous to meet Cal for dinner. What was wrong with me lately? Maybe I had the flu, or malaria. *I could only hope.*

Chapter 6

*B*y 6:45 PM my bed was covered in clothes and I still had no idea what to wear for my date with Cal. *Correction, this is not a date.* I just suddenly had no idea what to wear for a dinner non-date. I was holding my black fishnets and tossed them back on the bed. Fishnets after dark would scream slut. My scary tramp look during daylight was *ironic* but it took on a whole new meaning after dark. Great, what was I supposed to wear tonight? I opted for a black kimono top over red leggings with my black boots. *Too combat ninja?* Last minute I added a red and black choker and pulled my hair up with chopsticks. They were the kind from Yumm Mee take-away, not the fancy kind you buy at the mall, but they would have to do. There. Eat your heart out Calvin Miller. *Yup, there was something seriously wrong with me today.*

I came downstairs as my mom was coming through the front door. My parents worked really long hours during the week so we didn't usually have dinner together except on the weekends.

"Hi mom, I hope you don't mind but I have dinner plans tonight. Calvin's taking me to the Shalimar in Portsmouth," I said hoping that dropping Calvin's name would soften the fact I was going out on a school night. It seemed to do the trick.

"That's great sweetie, you look amazing," she said with an approving nod, "Cal's a lucky boy."

I thought about correcting her but was already running late and figured arguing over it being a non-date might cause her to make me stay home. I settled for blushing instead. *That was something I was going to do either way.*

Just then I heard Cal's truck pull into the driveway. Hoping to leave before anymore awkwardness, I ran for the door. "Bye mom!" I said as I opened the door.

"Bye sweetie," my mom answered before I closed the door, "Have fun!"

I was about to turn to walk down my front steps when I smelled wet dog. *Calvin.*

"You look amazing," Calvin said as he walked beside me to the truck.

"Um, thanks. You too," I stuttered as I he opened the passenger door for me. *You smell like wet dog.* I was starting to wonder if Calvin was taking in strays or working a side job at a pet grooming shop, but I didn't ask. *Maybe I don't want to know.*

"So the Shalimar?" he asked as we backed down my driveway.

His arm was over the back of the seat as he looked behind the truck and my heart started doing flip flops in my chest. *Yuki, get a grip.*

"Where else are we going to get Chanaa Masala?" I asked as an old argument began.

"Ew Yuki, why waste perfectly good Indian food on a chickpea dish?" Calvin replied, "Now *I* am going to order Lamb Jalfrazi." He actually looked like he was drooling.

Must be the reflection from the street lights.

"Emma would pass out if she were here," I tossed back at him.

"Emma isn't here," he said with a dangerous glint in his eye.

You got me there Calvin Miller.

"Plus, you said dinner was your treat so that means you are paying for a lamb to be slaughtered for my pleasure. That makes me some kind of god or something," he gloated showing that toothy grin that I was starting to think had a somewhat predatory look to it.

I kind of liked it. Oh man. Why do I have to have a bad boy complex? And why was Calvin Miller suddenly triggering it? I shivered and tried to change the subject. *You're in over your head Yuki.*

"So um, are we going to have to cross the bridge?" I asked lamely.

"No Yuki. I thought we'd swim," Calvin replied doing that eyebrow thing of his. "Of course we have to drive over the bridge."

"Oh," I whispered suddenly wishing we had picked somewhere else to go for dinner. That's me, tough combat ninja Yuki afraid of crossing over bridges. Someone once told me not to worry that I would outgrow my fear, but it hasn't happened yet.

Calvin seemed to tense up all of a sudden and then relax, "You can close your eyes the whole time we're on the bridge. I'll let you know when we've gone over it." He said it so softly and compassionately I was at a loss for words.

"Thanks. It means a lot," I hesitated for just a second and added, "Thanks Calvin." I was suddenly awash in wet dog smell, but I didn't have time to worry about it. I quickly squeezed my eyes shut and wrapped my arms around myself while inching down in my seat. *I had a bridge to cross.*

Chapter 7

Day three of school and the air was saturated with the smell of vinegar. I think Jackson was getting frustrated. *Could I blame him?* I had been distracted last night by thoughts of Calvin when I got home and hadn't gone online for any more research. Something was going on with Calvin, but I couldn't quite figure out what had changed about him. It was like someone had abducted my annoying friend and replaced him with a darker more secretive version. *He was still annoying though.* Maybe when I start my research on Jackson Green's family I should think about doing a covert search of Calvin's house. I could suggest doing the research at his place. We were on good terms since I stuffed him with Indian food last night. That boy really likes his meat, I thought with a shudder. *It was unnatural.*

Maybe I'd grab him an extra burger at lunch time to soften him up. It's not like I ever used my full lunch allowance on cafeteria food anyway. The only guaranteed vegetarian food was from the salad bar and I draw the line at getting my food from something that requires a sneeze guard. *So gross.* Emma says it's a conspiracy against non-flesh eaters. I'm not so sure, but today it just meant that my meal ticket was going to help me enlist Calvin's help after school. *Sorry cow and other meat byproducts.*

"Can you taste its fear?" Emma asked Calvin as he bit into his second burger. She was looking at him intently, probably revving up for one of her arguments against eating meat.

Calvin actually looked a little spooked by her question.

25

Could he taste its fear? I was glad to be eating fear-free celery sticks. "So Emma, you have a date for the dance?" I asked just to get her to change the subject. Was I actually trying to help Cal? *Maybe.*

"What? From this student body?" she guffawed. Seriously, she guffawed. It was kind of amazing. "There isn't a vegan among them," she said as she surveyed the boys in the cafeteria, "They all smell rancid to me," she said turning her attention back to us.

"Hey, I thought I was the one with smell issues," I laughed and grabbed another celery stick. Was she serious or was Emma making this up? I turned to Calvin to nudge him in the ribs but he was sitting there frozen mid-bite. *What was going on with him?*

"I'm serious Yuki. All that meat and dairy they eat just leaks out of their pores. It's disgusting," she said wrinkling her nose.

"So are you saying that since I eat dairy I stink too?" I asked wondering if I reeked of sour milk or something. I was tempted to sniff under my arms, but it didn't seem like a classy thing to do.

"You stink less than most," Emma said with a smile.

Was that a compliment? My friends were really starting to bug me today. Emma was looking smug and Calvin had gone from startled to contemplative. I really wasn't sure what was on his mind. He was rubbing his upper arm over and over like he was trying to reassure himself. *About what?* Plus I wasn't sure if it was all of the talk about smells, but I was starting to catch a whiff of that wet dog smell again. *Weird.*

"I'm taking my slightly stinky self to the computer lab. Maybe I can find something out about Mr. Green during my free period," I said as I stood up to leave. Lunch was almost over anyway. I might as well get to work on helping my ghostly shadow. *Why did he have to smell like vinegar?* I wondered for the millionth time today.

"You never told me who you were going with," Emma said as she came up behind me tossing her juice can into the recycling bin, "Do you have a date for the homecoming dance?"

I glanced across the cafeteria to where Calvin was still sitting. "I was thinking about asking Garrett to the dance," I said surprising myself with my boldness. Right at that moment a dark look crossed Calvin's face and he stopped rubbing his arm. He thrust himself upright with both palms flat on the lunch table and glared at me through his shaggy bangs. *What was his problem?* There was no way he could hear my conversation with Emma since he was on the opposite end of a noisy cafeteria. I had lost my bravado though and sheepishly looked back at Emma. "Well, I might maybe possibly perhaps ask him. I'm not really sure yet." *Way to be decisive Yuki.*

"Good luck with that," Emma said sarcastically and turned gracefully to leave.

I scanned the cafeteria one more time for Calvin, but he appeared to have vanished. I pulled my backpack further up my shoulder and headed for the doors closest to the computer lab. *Looks like it's just you and me Vinegar Dude.*

Chapter 8

*I*n the computer lab I was chewing on my second pen and typing away with my overly chewed manicure. *Oh yah, that's attractive.* I would just have to repaint my nails over the weekend. Right now I needed to focus on helping Jackson Green and doing some super secret snooping on Calvin. I had already sent a copy of Jackson's obituary and a few maps and satellite images of the farm to the printer. I was just about to open up another window to do a search on Calvin Miller when a voice beside me made me jump.

"Did you know that every time a fly lands it either defecates or lays an egg?" Calvin asked while looking pointedly at the chewed pen in my mouth.

That's why I hate you Calvin Miller.

"You're beginning to sound like Emma," I said bluntly looking to the stack of papers in his hands.

"That's probably because she was the one who told me that in the first place," he said with a laugh. He leaned up against the lab table and shuffled the stack of papers.

Holy heck. I was so glad there wasn't anything pertaining to my super-secret snooping in that stack.

Raising one eyebrow he lifted the stack of papers and asked, "Why the maps to the farm? You think I'd forget how to get us there?"

Us?

"I didn't know if you'd be busy later so I printed those for Emma," I said thinking that I wouldn't have to ask for a ride if I had my license. I was the last of my friends to get a driver's license, but my inability to drive over bridges wasn't scoring me any points on that front. Plus, what would I do if I were hit with a smell impression in the middle of driving. It was potentially dangerous and I was beginning to learn that, though it may sound cool, *Danger* was not my middle name. *Speaking of danger.*

"Um, Calvin I was thinking this search might get, you know, dangerous. It might be better if you came along with me instead of Emma," I said trying not to sound too pleading. I was not going to beg Calvin Miller to drive me to the farm. *No way.*

"I'm surprised you don't ask Garrett Hamlin," he said sulkily looking down at his feet.

For a second I couldn't quite catch my breath. *There was that wet dog smell again too.* He must have taken my non-answer as a rejection because he suddenly tossed the stack of papers on the table next to my keyboard and loped across the room in three easy strides. *Son of a dung beetle.* I quickly shut down the computer and tossed the papers into my open backpack. I ran for the hallway, my chunky boots clomping and squeaking loudly on the linoleum floor. Which way had he gone and how had he moved so silently? *Like a cat...or a wolf.*

I turned left on impulse and started down the hallway towards our lockers. I remembered learning the word left in Italian and how the word sinistra sounded like the word sinister. Emma and I had spent the day looking up old beliefs about left handed people being evil and she went into a major frenzy about human rights abuses in the dark ages. Yup, I was heading along the sinistra path since it seemed to match the direction this day was going. *Maybe I should have turned right.*

As I walked past the boy's bathroom, just before our row of lockers, I heard a whimpering sound. *Oh no. Please no.* Was that Cal? If it was, did that mean Calvin Miller actually had a crush on me? Taking a deep breath and trying to clear my mind the way the yoga instructor taught us in the class Calvin had taken me to last year, I prepared myself to call his name. "Cal? Um, you in there?" I called tentatively. The sound echoed a bit and I cleared my throat to try again. *Less wimpy this time Yuki.*

"Calvin?" I called a bit louder this time. O.k. that was better but this was still awkward with a capital A.

"Mmm," he answered.

It was really more of a sound than a word, but now I knew for sure he was in the boy's bathroom. *Crying over me.*

"So uh, this is probably the most epically bad time to ask this but would you like to go to the homecoming dance with me?" I asked in my wimpy whisper voice. Cal may be a huge pain in my backside, but he was also one of my best friends. I realized that I had been pretty selfish lately focusing on my smell impressions and obsessing over starting senior year and had managed to hurt his feelings. I owed it to Calvin to try to make it up to him. That's all this was, right? *So why was asking him to the dance so difficult?*

I didn't want him to think it was just a pity date, though, so I tried to keep talking. "Remember that fab corset dress I found in Salem? The one I've been dying to wear?" I said sounding more normal. Keep it up Yuki. It was easier to talk about dresses than about why he was crying in the bathroom. "Well, I was hoping to wear it to the dance. So will you? Go to the dance with me?" I asked hoping he'd say yes.

"You don't really want to go with me," he said sniffing a bit, but sounding more like the normal Calvin.

"Of course I do!" I said putting my hands on my hips and suddenly realizing that I did want to go to the dance with Cal. "I want a date that will look just as fantabulous as that dress," I said. *Now where had that come from?* He would look pretty amazing dressed up for the dance. Maybe I could even talk him into just a teensy bit of eyeliner to show off those gorgeous blue eyes of his. *Probably not.*

I heard water running and the paper towel dispenser clanking and the next second Calvin was standing in front

31

of me. His left hand was rubbing his right bicep again and he looked a bit self conscious, but he wasn't crying. In fact, he looked pretty amazing. When I cry my face goes all puffy and covered in red blotches. Calvin's face was still tanned and perfect with shiny wet eyelashes and sparkling blue eyes. *I could get lost in those eyes.*

I must have been staring at him a bit too long because he took a shaky breath and raked his hand through his shaggy brown hair. His gorgeous silky, so totally not gelled into a helmet, hair. *Wow, what was up with me?* I suddenly wanted to run my fingers through his hair so bad my hands flexed. I quickly stuffed them into my pockets. Maybe vinegar and wet dog was an aphrodisiac. *Who would have suspected?*

"So do you still want me to pick you up later?" Calvin asked.

Later? I was having a total brain freeze. *What was later?*

"To go out to the Green farm?" he asked clarifying and helping my brain resume function.

"Oh. Yah. Totally. That would be great," I stuttered. *Smooth one Yuki.* Then in one lightening fast move I stepped forward, gave Cal a hug, and ran down the hall to my locker. For once I had left Calvin Miller at a loss for words.

Chapter 9

*A*s soon as I dumped my backpack on my bed after school, I grabbed my phone and called Emma. "I have a date for the homecoming dance," I blurted out before she could say anything. I was so excited it came out all one word. *Ihaveadateforthehomecomingdance.*

"I should charge you both counseling fees," she replied dryly.

"What?" I exclaimed wondering what she was talking about. Had Calvin called her already?

"I knew you and Calvin were going to hook up," she said smugly. "You two are perfect for each other by the way."

"Uh, well I'm not sure you could say we've hooked up, but we are going to the dance together," I said wondering what Calvin had said to Emma. Maybe she'd spill if I gave her a few details of my own. "I hugged him!" I blurted.

"Yah girl, I know. You nearly put the poor boy into cardiac arrest," she said starting to laugh. "Is there a reason though why you suddenly changed your mind and had to ask Calvin to the dance while he was in the bathroom? Some secret toilet fetish I should know about?" she asked teasingly.

Son of a dung beetle. Calvin had talked to her first and I'm sure he didn't mention that he was crying in the bathroom. So I had asked a guy out to the dance while he was in the bathroom. It sounded weird even to me *and I was there.*

"O.k. then All Knowing One, what should I wear? Calvin is picking me up in an hour to go do recon at the

Green farm and I have no idea how to dress," I said starting to worry.

"Yuki, he likes you for who you are. Just be yourself. You know, wear lots of black and a pair of your big chunky boots. He'll be swooning." The last she said dramatically. "Lip gloss," she added, "You want to look like you--but kissable."

With a laugh Emma hung up leaving me staring at my reflection in the mirror and wondering if I even owned lip gloss. I looked down at my hands and decided to touch up my nail polish instead. *Maybe he'd want to at least hold my hand.*

Chapter 10

I ran out to meet Calvin in the driveway as soon as his truck came to a stop. Usually I make him come get me, but I wasn't quite ready to be alone with him in my bedroom. Things that seemed totally normal yesterday suddenly felt very, very weird. Tingling with excitement, and feeling hopeful that we'd turn up some clues today, I jumped up on the passenger side running board. Calvin was already leaning over to open my door. He stayed leaning towards me as I pulled myself inside the truck. The truck was awash with the wet dog smell again, but I barely noticed. Calvin was looking at me intently through his shaggy bangs. *Intense.* The word just took on a whole new meaning for me. I'd never been looked at that way before. It was thrilling and just a tiny bit scary. I wanted to check how I looked in the mirror but I didn't dare break his gaze.

"Yuki," he said as I watched his Adam's apple rise and lower, "would you like to go out with me?"

His eyes never left my face as I whispered, "Yes."

His face lit up with a roguish smile and he lifted my chin with one hand and came so close that his next words moved against my lips, "me too," he said and kissed me on the lips. *I think I'm falling in love with you Calvin Miller.*

Cal was the first to break away and running his hand through his hair he moved back behind the wheel. He started the truck and we headed out to the Green farm. I sat there a little stunned, with a big stupid grin on my face. It was all I could do to not bounce up and down in the seat. I looked out the window as the trees spun by

35

and thought I might actually be in Heaven. For once in my life things seemed to be going in the right direction.

As we pulled onto the gravel road that led to the farm, we talked about the information we had found on the internet. So far we didn't have a lot to go on, but we both thought it was notable that none of Jackson Green's sons had worked for the farm. They had all gone on to work professional jobs in Portland and Boston. The death of all three sons in a boating accident also seemed suspicious and we speculated that they may have been cut out of their father's will and trying to steal the inheritance money. Calvin had also found that Jackson Green and his wife Grace had been very active with environmental charities and had donated large portions of the farm's recent profits to organizations that promoted organic farming and environmental awareness. Perhaps the sons were afraid that all of the money they longed for would be given away to charity? It was all just wild conjecture, but it did provide possible motive.   Motive for what was the big question.

"Do you think Mr. Green could have been murdered?" feeling a bit queasy as I said it. The thought of smelling a dead man was bad enough, but to think he might be the spirit of someone who was murdered was almost too horrible to consider.

Calvin nodded slowly. "It's a possibility, but it may not have been like that. It could have been an accident or he may just have passed away of old age. But don't worry. We'll find out what happened and help his spirit find peace."

I looked out over the beautiful orchards and farm fields and for the first time I really believed it. How could we not find peace for him in this beautiful place?

I pulled out the satellite maps and colored pencils. My plan was to mark in red places on the map that differed from what we could see, since the images were taken over a year ago and any differences might indicate recent changes to the landscape. We were also going to mark in green places that looked suspicious or that might be a good hiding place for the inheritance. My hope was to find a location that had potential for a hiding spot and had been recently changed. If we could find such a spot, we would then mark it with an X. *Like hunting for buried treasure.*

There was a smell to the west, out by the orchard, that smelled like rotting garbage and manure. At first I wondered if it might be another smell impression, but when I looked over at Calvin his nose was wrinkled in disgust. Good. If he smelled it too, then it must be some kind of fertilizer or something. *Thank goodness.* I didn't think I could deal with another haunting right now. I followed Cal as he headed away from the smell.

After two hours of hiking around the property, we both had maps covered in red and green pencil but not one mark that overlapped. Grabbing water bottles from the truck, we started again in the opposite field. Calvin was definitely grossed out by the smell and after a few minutes of searching went back to his truck. When he returned a minute later, he had a handkerchief over the lower half of his face.

"About to raid a stage coach?" I asked trying not to laugh since that would make me taste the garbage manure smell.

"Calvin the Bandit at your service," he replied bowing low at the waist.

I started to laugh again and had to bite my lip to keep my mouth closed. "I think I'm actually glad that everything smells like vinegar," I quipped. In fact the vinegar smell was suddenly getting stronger. "Uh Cal, I think we're heading in the right direction," I said. Goosebumps raised on my arms and neck and my head was flooded with the smell of vinegar. I suddenly felt light headed and a buzzing sound started whirring in my ears. I went to take a step and suddenly didn't know where my feet were.

"Yuki? Yuki! Are you alright? Can you hear me?" Calvin asked worriedly. He was kneeling on the ground holding me sitting upright.

I must have fallen or passed out. "Mmm, yah. I think so," I mumbled feeling fuzzy. His blue eyes suddenly came into focus and I felt like I could breathe. "Can you help me up? I think we're really close," I said as he carefully helped me to my feet. Calvin was hovering as I turned in a slow circle to get a reading. The smell and the new tingling sensation seemed to be coming from the northwest. "That way," I pointed and we started up the hill.

We finally came to a heap of refuse that I guess was the Green farm compost pile. I looked at the satellite map to confirm my suspicion. This compost heap wasn't on the satellite map. *It was new.* My excitement was dimmed only when I realized what that meant. We were going to have to dig in this thing for clues. I turned to Cal to see that he had come to the same conclusion. I could have sworn I heard a whimper escape his lips. This sucks eggs. *What else is new?*

I was suddenly glad that I had worn my shiny vinyl club boots. The deep tread would be a pain to scrape out later, but I would stay a lot cleaner than Calvin. He had on a pair of sandals and I shuddered at the thought of decomposing vegetable matter squishing between his toes. I tied the ends of my skirt up like puffy pantaloons and dug the garden trowel I had brought with me out of my backpack. Calvin looked even more upset as he pulled a spork from his school bag. *Trowel envy Calvin Miller?* Feeling just a bit smug I pulled another small shovel from my bag. It was a kid's beach shovel, but it was a million times bigger than his spork.

"Here you go Cal. You'd make a terrible pirate you know," I said laughing as I handed him the shovel and then wincing at the foul taste.

"I told you Yuki. I'm Calvin the Bandit," he said primly as he bent down to start digging. I had to bite my lip to stifle another laugh as we both set to work on the compost heap.

Chapter 11

After what seemed like decades, but was probably just an hour, my trowel hit something. The sound of metal scraping on metal carried over the buzzing of flies and Calvin and I smiled for the first time since we had started digging.

"Please say that is our buried treasure," Calvin moaned. He had turned an unhealthy shade of green and looked like he was going to be sick.

I was tempted to tease him about his wimpy stomach, but decided it was unfair. How was I to know how bad it really smelled out here? I was in a perpetual cloud of vinegar smell thanks to Jackson's ghost.

I carefully wiggled the metal box until I was able to pull it out of the heap with a sucking sound. I started to stumble back when Calvin caught my arm. "Thanks. This is one place I really do not want to fall on my butt," I said.

I figured we had suffered enough, so I started walking away from the heap and toward the truck. Before getting in I poured the rest on my water bottle over my hands and then grabbed the hand sanitizer I never leave home without. Calvin looked at it longingly and I handed it over to him. "Is it alright to get in your truck?" I asked Cal suddenly realizing just how filthy we were.

"Sure. Just a sec," he said as he ran over to the back of the truck. He came back with towels which he threw over the bench seat of the truck. "All set," he said and stepped back.

I didn't want to get caught near the farm with the box, so I suggested we wait until we were back on the highway before I tried to open it. The box appeared to be a metal toolbox with a latch but no lock. Once we were cruising on the highway I opened the latch. The lid fell back against the tops of my knees as I stared at the contents. Calvin was dividing his attention between the box and the road, but I could see the look of relief on his face. "We did it," I said. The box was filled with papers in clear plastic bags. They looked like legal documents, deeds and maybe even a will, and in the bottom were stacks of cash. *Buried treasure.*

Calvin reached over and took my hand, holding it for a moment and then giving it a squeeze. "You did it Yuki," he said proudly, "Your power is kind of amazing."

My power. I had never really thought of it that way before. It was something I was still trying to get used to and so far it had just been aggravating. If we could figure out what Jackson Green's ghost wanted us to do with the contents of this box, then we could put his soul to rest. His spirit could be at peace. Maybe my ability to smell the dead wasn't so bad after all.

"Is Mr. Green's ghost still here?" Calvin asked.

"Yes, but I think you're right. With these papers we should be able to figure out why he's bound here. The reason why he can't rest," I said. Looking inside the box I could see that it would take us a while to read through all of the documents. We pulled up to my house and Calvin walked me to the door. "You want to come inside and start reading through these now?" I asked holding up the metal box.

"No thanks," he said looking chagrined, "I really need to go take a shower."

"Right, me too," I said and started to turn to go inside.

"Yuki?" Calvin asked.

"Yah?" I asked turning back to him.

"Thanks for giving me a chance," he said and smiling his toothy grin he started walking back to his truck.

Who else is going to dig through a compost heap with me? It must be love. *Maybe, just maybe, it is.*

Chapter 12

I woke up Saturday morning shaking and drenched in sweat. When I went to bed last night I was looking forward to solving my ghost problem and seeing Calvin. Due to the Labor Day holiday our first week of school was just three days. After such an exciting day Friday, I was thinking about spending time with Cal over the weekend when I drifted off to sleep. That doesn't explain my dream though. Dream? *It was a nightmare.* In my dream a weathered man and a huge silver gray wolf stood together beneath a full moon. They were atop a hill and no matter which direction I looked, in the distance I saw the devastation of severe drought. Looking back at the man and the wolf I saw the tears in their eyes evaporate on the wind. *It was too dry even for tears to fall.*

Then, as is often the way of dreams, I stood in my bedroom looking out over my yard as a full moon washed everything a ghostly gray. I heard the howl of a wolf then found myself in a long hallway and saw an elderly man in overalls walking towards a white light. He smiled at me and then pointed over my shoulder. I turned to look behind me and a huge silver wolf, like the one that had been on the drought scarred hill, stood facing me in the hall. He was beautiful, though his eyes looked sad. The wolf began scratching at a red door to my left and whimpering to be let out. I went to open the door, but as the door knob started to turn I woke up. *What did it mean?*

The dream left me worn out and part of me wanted to try going back to sleep to find out what lay beyond the red door. Maybe I could ask Calvin about it later. He was interested in dream interpretation and had bought a few books on dream symbols on our last trip to Salem. What was it Cal said you're supposed to do first? Keep a dream diary? I found a sales flyer for Manic Panic hair dye. "Sorry Tish and Snooky," I muttered as I wrote silver wolf, full moon, hallway, light, and red door along the edge of the flyer. I put my new dream diary on the night stand beside my bed and placed the pen on top. I could always use it as a backup excuse to have Calvin come over later. I floated down the stairs to have breakfast with my parents, banishing thoughts of wolves and tears to the shadows.

Chapter 13

*H*is phone just rang and rang. I had been trying to
reach Calvin for hours. His cell phone went immediately
to voicemail and his home phone just rang endlessly.
Where was he? It was possible his parents had taken him
somewhere for the weekend. His family seemed to love
the outdoors and often went on hiking and camping trips.
But wouldn't he have called? I was trying to think of
reasons for Calvin's absence that didn't involve him
injured in a ditch somewhere. Hoping that he had gone to
visit a shrine where cell phones, and often speaking
aloud, were prohibited, I closed my phone.

With a sigh I turned my attention back to the metal
box. The legal language was a bit archaic, but after a few
hours of reading, and a couple of internet searches to
figure out what certain legalese meant, I had a fairly clear
picture of the events surrounding Jackson Green's death.
We would probably never know for sure what happened
on the day of his death, but it looked as though Jackson
had been aware that his days were numbered. He had
made numerous revisions to his will in the last months of
his life with a clause to cut his sons out of it just days
before their boat accident. It seemed like more than just
coincidence.

What was I supposed to do next? That was where
things became murky. Jackson's final will and testament
left the farm and controlling shares of farm stocks to his
wife Grace. The remainder of his stock portfolio, the cash
in the box, and his other land holdings were to go to
environmental charities. The details were all in his will
and in a few letters of correspondence with staff in the

fundraising offices. The only thing that held me back from posting these to his wife and the charities was a question that had been nagging me since the beginning. If murder had been committed, then how involved was Jackson Green's wife? I was going to have to experiment with my smell impressions before I made a final decision about the contents of the box. *I was going to have to pay Grace Green a visit.*

After checking my phone again for messages, I finally gave up on waiting for Calvin to call and went to sleep. I was soon dreaming about sitting across from him on my bed with the metal box set between us on the comforter. Dream Calvin then stood and walked in a circle to be suddenly replaced by a large wolf that lay on the floor beside my bed. The metal box then burst open and hundreds of butterflies flew into a bright light shining above my room. Captivated by the light I reached upward and began to stand. I was pulled back to the bed and I looked down to see the wolf holding the edge of my shirt in his teeth. "Thank you for protecting me," my dream self told the wolf. I suddenly bolted awake to the sound of howling outside my window. It was hours before I finally drifted back to a dreamless sleep.

Chapter 14

I only had my dream diary for two days and I had already failed to use it. I was trying to remember my dream from last night but it was no use. It was like trying to grasp at smoke. *That's why people keep dream diaries.*

I closed my eyes and tried again. Sitting crossed legged, the lotus position Cal would call it, I leaned against the pillows propped at the top of my bed and slowed my breathing. I tried to picture my dream as something tangible that I could grab hold of. I reached my mental fingers out toward the dream remnants and my phone beeped. I jumped and hit my head on the headboard. *Ouch.* I scrambled to uncross my tangled legs and grab my phone off the nightstand.

It was a text from Calvin. I hit view message to see his question, "R u home?"

"Yes where r u?" I texted back.

"Can I come over?" he asked.

You didn't answer my question Calvin Miller.

"OK," I texted back. I couldn't decide if I was happy or angry. Judging by the butterflies in my stomach I was mostly nervous. *Butterflies.* Wasn't there something about butterflies in my dream? I was interrupted by a knock at the front door. "I guess I know where Calvin is," I muttered as I went to let him in. He could have at least given me a few minutes to freshen up. *Boys.*

"Hey," I said as I opened the door.

"Hey," Calvin whispered back. He started rubbing his arm then stuffed his hands in his pockets only to switch back to rubbing his arm again. Cal was also shuffling his feet back and forth and looking everywhere but at me.

Nervous much?

"Uh, come on up," I said and started up the stairs to my room.

When we reached my room I threw my butt onto the bed and crossed my arms. I was still a little angry about his disappearing act. Calvin hovered in the doorway and finally came in to stand as far away from me as he could and still be in the bedroom. *Do I smell or something?* His standoffishness was making me even angrier. Calvin kept fidgeting like he was uncomfortable in his own skin. He repeatedly glanced back and forth between the door and the window like he was looking for a way out.

Was he having second thoughts about the two of us dating? *Please no, not that.* Something was definitely going on and his behavior only made sense if he thought our going out was a mistake. Cal was probably worried about ruining our friendship and was trying to come up with a way to break up with me. Well, I wasn't going to make it easy on him. If that's what he came here to do, then he would have to man up and say it himself. *Don't make me hate you Calvin Miller.*

"So where were you all weekend?" I sniped at him. It came out sounding rude but my feelings were too hurt to care.

"In the woods," he said sullenly. Not "hiking with my parents" or "camping with my family" but "in the woods." Something about the way he said it sounded ominous and maybe a little angry.

"I missed you," I said quietly. Where had that come from? *Way to be tough Yuki.* Now he was probably going to think I was too needy and run for the hills. *Or the woods.*

"Me too Yuki. I," he said stepping forward. But as he came within inches of me he retreated to the doorway. "I'm sorry. I can't do this," he said sounding out of breath, "It's too soon."

48

Too soon for what?

"My dad was right," he muttered, "I'm not ready." He started to walk out the door.

Out of my life.

"Cal, please don't go!" a strangled voice cried out.

My voice.

Calvin paused and without turning to look at me said, "Don't give up on me Yuki. Not yet." Then he ran down the stairs and out to his truck. I heard the driver's door slam shut and the engine roar.

Don't give up on me Yuki his voice echoed in my head. Those words gave me hope but I still grabbed the beetle plushie off the floor and, squeezing it tight to my chest, sobbed into my pillow. It was not too dry for my tears to fall.

Chapter 15

*M*onday had been an out service day, with the school week resuming Tuesday. This meant that I had all of Monday to cry before returning to school. *Where I would have to face him.* I hadn't heard from Calvin again since our brief talk in my bedroom yesterday so I didn't know what to expect. Would he a) apologize, b) act like nothing was wrong, c) break up with me, or d) make it up to me with a kiss? I was hoping he would go for option-d, perhaps with a bit of option-a as well. *Grovel and kiss me you fool.*

I hadn't seen Calvin yet and when I walked into the physics class we had together his desk was depressingly empty. I tried not to read too much into his absence but the empty desk haunted me all through class. *Maybe he's just coming in late today.* If that were the case, I would make sure to see him at lunch. If he was in the building at noon, he would be in the cafeteria. No one would get between Calvin and his burgers. That boy had a crazy healthy appetite.

Lunch was even more depressing. There was no sign of Cal and without anyone to tease about the injustices of meat processing Emma sat picking at her orange wedges without her usual enthusiasm.

"This sucks," Emma finally stated. "I need a victim and no offense Yuki, but your carrot sticks are lacking in controversy." She raised one eyebrow at my bag of carrot sticks and for a moment my stomach twisted at the memory of Calvin pulling the same face just a few days before.

"I did hear someone once claim that carrots had nervous systems and so could therefore feel pain," I said trying to keep the conversation going. I knew I was desperate when Emma's rants were a necessary distraction from my thoughts.

"Really?" she asked hopefully. Both of Emma's eyebrows were raised now and the hopeful look on her face was kind of funny.

"Mm hmm, though the information hasn't been verified," I added trying to sound serious. Emma was big on scientific proof for her arguments.

"This sucks," she moaned again and put her face down on her hands. "Where is Cal when I need him?" she whined.

My thoughts exactly.

"So Emma, want to go on a spying trip after school?" I asked.

"Like double-oh-seven?" she asked picking her head up off the table.

"Totally," I replied. "There may even be multiple counts of bee slavery on the premises."

"Really? I'm so there," she answered.

Thank goodness for bee oppression.

"Should I dress up? Do you think there will be any hot double agents?" she asked hopefully.

Thinking of Jared Zempter I shuddered. *More like Frankenstein's monster.* "Maybe. Bring lip gloss," I said and forced a laugh.

Emma waved as she shoved an orange wedge into her mouth and ran to class. *Looks like she got her appetite back.* If I couldn't get my boyfriend back today, then maybe I could settle for getting rid of my ghost.

Chapter 16

*E*mma pulled her car onto the gravel road and I told her to pull us to the side and park. When we got out and stretched she looked from the sign for Green Orchards Apple Cider Vinegar Company with its *Always natural. Now certified organic* claim and back to me. She was looking at me like I had three heads.

"What?" I asked rolling my eyes.

"Yuki. This is an organic farm. Please tell me we are not doing some covert raid on an *organic farm!*" Emma demanded.

"But they're the evil overlords of bees," I said lamely.

Son of a dung beetle. This wasn't going as planned, though I had to admit that I didn't actually have much of a plan. "Emma look, I just need to go up to the main house and get a sense of the old lady inside. If she seems like a nice grandmother type and invites us in for cookies, then I can fix my ghost problem. If she is more of an evil stepmother who murders her sons and husband type, then we can run like crazy back to your car. Either way you can write an article for the school paper about how they oppress bees and steal their honey," I pleaded. "It would help to raise awareness," I added hopefully.

Emma crossed her arms but agreed. "Alright, but you owe me one," she said as we walked towards the house on the hill.

Grace Green turned out to be an energetic woman who my mom would say has lots of spunk. She was dressed in blue jeans, a flannel shirt, and a sun hat that left a cross-hatch of shadow across her tanned face. Grace was busy working in her herb garden at the side of the house, but stopped when we approached. We had explained that we were working on an article for our school paper and Emma went on to ask her questions about raising honey bees. I was doing my best to observe Grace while trying to sense any difference in her husband's smell impression. *This is harder than I thought.*

I wasn't sure how I was supposed to get a fix on a ghost's intention from a smell. When we were looking for clues I had known that we were getting warmer when the smell became stronger. But would a strong smell around Grace mean she was the one to give the inheritance to, or just the opposite? Would it mean he loved his wife, or that his wife was a cold hearted murderer?

Emma and Grace were talking about pollination, and I was about to give up my search, when a black and yellow butterfly landed on one of the plants in Grace's herb garden. *Black and yellow butterfly.*

"Mrs. Green," I said startling them both by finally speaking, "What kind of plant is this one here?"

For a moment a look of horror crossed her face but then she answered, "Oh that silly thing? You don't want to touch that one dear. It's for constipation."

I pulled my hand back, but thoughts were racing though my head. I was also overwhelmed with the smell of vinegar. Emma seemed to get the drift that things had just gone in a weird direction and asked if we could see the hives before leaving. Grace looked relieved to have us out of her garden and on our way. Before walking away though, I bent down pretending to tie my boot laces. I snapped a few photos of the plant with my cell phone and ran to catch up with Emma and a woman who I was beginning to suspect of murder.

Chapter 17

*E*mma and I walked casually back to her car trying not to burst with excitement.

"Ohmygosh!" Emma blurted as soon as we pulled onto the highway ramp.

"I second that emotion," I said trying to calm my rapid heartbeat and shaking hands.

"I think I just scored the best story for the school paper," Emma exclaimed.

"Wait a sec. What?" I asked suddenly wondering if we were on the same page.

"That woman is the queen bee overlord. It will make the best headline for the school paper," Emma said obviously excited.

"So what you're saying is that you're just psyched to have scored an interview with a mastermind of bee oppression?" I asked incredulously.

"Well duh, what were you talking about," Emma shot back.

Patience Yuki.

"I was talking about finding out Grace Green is probably a murderer," I blurted out defensively. *So much for patience.*

"Yah girl, a murderer of defenseless bees," Emma said.

I couldn't tell if she was teasing me or serious. *Probably serious.*

"Emma, do you know much about plants?" I asked hoping she might be able to help me identify the plant from my photos.

"I know I like to eat them if they're chemical free," she said with an evil laugh.

I sighed in exasperation.

"What?" asked Emma. "I'm hungry." Right then Emma's stomach growled out loud and we couldn't help but laugh.

"I'm hiding my African violets when we get to my house," I said and we laughed again.

We were silent the rest of the way home. *Well, except for Emma's stomach.*

When we reached my house Emma had decided to go home where her mom already had a dinner ready. I told her I had research to do and would see her tomorrow at school. I went up to my room and downloaded the pictures from the Green farm off my phone onto my laptop. Zooming in I could tell they didn't look like the herbs I was familiar with like rosemary, oregano, mint, sage, and thyme. My next step was to try searching for the plant on the Internet. I tried "green oval leaves," "bell shaped purple flowers," and "poison" for a search. After a few useless searches, I found pictures of a plant that matched the one in Grace Green's herb garden. It had the same dark, dingy purple bell shaped flowers and deeply veined green oval leaves. *Son of a dung beetle.* The plant was listed as *Atropa Belladonna,* what is commonly known as Deadly Nightshade.

Chapter 18

I went to bed that night feeling spooked. I knew it was probably silly to worry about Grace Green coming after me in my sleep, but I still felt uneasy. I pulled a box down from the top of my closet and pushed things around until I found the sleigh bells I had used to decorate my room last Christmas. *Better than nothing.* I grabbed a hair ribbon off my vanity and strung a few of the bells across the ribbon then tied the ribbon across my windows. I grabbed the largest bell and with a piece of string and a bent thumbtack hung it above my door. Similar to the gift shops on Main Street, the bell would jangle if anyone opened the door while I slept. Feeling satisfied that at least no one would be sneaking up on me, I crawled into bed.

Sleep, however, wasn't as easy as my new alarm system. Every time I closed my eyes I would picture Calvin leaning in to kiss me. I would force my eyes open and try to think about anything but Calvin, yet questions continued to spin around my head. *Where had he gone? What was he not ready for? Why did he have to leave?*

I must have finally fallen asleep because I was standing beneath a full moon on the drought stricken hilltop from my previous dream. *You're not in Kansas anymore Yuki.* There was the silhouette of a man standing before me against the light of the moon and a huge silver wolf lay at my feet. Having the wolf with me made me feel safe, though I realized that this wasn't very logical. He was larger than any dog I had ever seen. His silver fur reflected the moonlight and seemed to dance as a breeze rolled across the hilltop. This land seemed to emanate sadness and I remembered the man's tears when he had appeared in my previous dream.

"Spirit Walker," said the man though his mouth didn't appear to move. "Bringer of the dead. There is much to tell you and little time," he said and his words echoed inside my head.

I nodded and reached down to sink my hand into the wolf's fur. I wasn't sure what the man needed to say, but understood that our time was limited.

"You must help the lost find their way. You must lead your people to the river of light. Too many walk the in-between worlds. Too many souls are lost," the man said pausing to look at the wolf at my feet. *My wolf.*

"Your path will not be an easy one. You have been granted a guardian and now both of your destinies are bound together. If you lose your way, listen for the howl of the wolf and in all things follow your heart," the man said as he began to fade.

"Wait! I don't understand," I yelled. The wind was rising creating a roaring dust cloud between us.

The man reached out, placing his hand on my shoulder, his voice again in my head, "Keep your feet on the path of healing. Help the lost ones find their way. You must be the flame in the darkness."

Before the wind tore him from me I looked down at his arm. His bicep was ringed in a black tattoo of a wolf chasing a hawk. I realized as I drifted out of the dream that the hawk was also chasing the wolf. Then there were no thoughts at all.

Chapter 19

After a long day of school filled with flitting images of wolves and lost souls, I was exhausted. I sat on the edge of my bed and grabbed an old notebook off my bookcase. It was already half used but there was plenty of room for a dream diary. I tore out the used pages and wrote Dream Diary across the cover. *There that's better.* After this last dream, I had to replace my hair dye flyer with something larger. These new dreams were confusing and I was determined to figure out what they meant.

The black and yellow butterfly in Grace Green's garden had seemed like more than a coincidence and the man in last night's dream talked about helping lost souls into the light. *That's what I'm doing right?*

I dialed Cal's number and it went to voicemail. *Again.* He still wasn't answering or returning my calls. Fine, I would just go to him. I grabbed a black scarf and arm warmers and stuffed them into my bag. It was still warm out, but the evenings were starting to get chilly. I lifted my bag and with a shrug tossed the dream diary in too.

Without a car I had to walk the three miles to Calvin's house. I could have called Emma for a ride, but I needed time to think and the walk helped to clear my head. When I was about a block away I heard music blasting and as his house came into sight I could tell the garage door was wide open. As I got closer I could see Calvin lifting weights in the open garage. *Shirtless.* His arms were bulging and for a moment I was dumbstruck. *When did you get so hot Calvin Miller?*

Glad he was facing away from me I tried to stop the blood from rushing to my face. Yoga breathing wasn't working. *Maybe I should have paid more attention in class.* I could feel my face turning a brighter shade of red with every thrust of the weights. I started walking forward again wondering how I was going to get Calvin's attention with the music blaring. Just then he stopped. He hadn't turned around yet but somehow he had known I was there.

It was then that I saw it. I was still focused on Calvin's flexed arms, how could I not be, when I saw a tattoo ringed his right bicep. I knew he didn't have a tattoo earlier this summer which meant the tattoo had to be new. *Weird.* Cal never seemed interested in tattoos or piercings before. It looked good on him though. *Really good.*

Calvin set the weights down slowly and walked to the stereo on the workbench. He turned the music off, but still hadn't turned around to face me. The silence felt like a wall between us and I was tired of his hiding.

"Calvin Bartholomew Miller," I yelled at his back. "You haven't been to school and I was worried about you. You disappeared and you don't return my calls," I said my voice getting shaky. *Son of a dung beetle.* If he didn't turn around soon and say something I was going to cry. *Don't make me cry Calvin Miller.*

"I miss you. You're standing right in front of me and I miss you," I choked and turned to leave. He hadn't said anything. I was leaving and he wasn't trying to stop me. *This must be what it feels like when your heart is breaking.* My feet felt frozen to the ground and yet all I wanted to do was run. Run as far away as I could and never come back.

Then his arms were surrounding me. I hadn't heard him walk up behind me, but suddenly he had his arms wrapped around me and his warm chest pressed against my back. Calvin buried his face into my hair and then his right arm shifted and his tattoo was just inches from my face.

Then I passed out.

"Yuki?" a voice called to me.

I felt like I was sinking deeper and deeper.

"Yuki?" the voice called again.

Cal? It couldn't be Calvin. He was avoiding me and I was here sinking into the nice warm water.

"Yuki! Wake up," the voice pleaded.

Suddenly I remembered going to Calvin's house and trying to talk to him. *Oh why did I say all those corny things to him?* I remembered trying to leave and his arms around me. *Oh son of a dung beetle, his arm.* His arm had a tattoo similar to the one on the man in my dream.

Suddenly I pushed up from the darkness and was awake. "Cal?" I asked.

"Yuki, are you alright?" he asked with relief on his face.

"Cal, show me your arm," I said trying to sit upright. The world was still moving a little and there were still shadows on the edges of my vision. "Calvin Miller, show me your right arm," I said more forcefully.

He looked confused, and a bit embarrassed, but he showed me his right arm. "It's just a tattoo. No big," he said trying to make light of it.

Now that I had a close-up look at his tattoo, I could tell what was different from the one on the man in my dream. In my dream the man had a tattoo of a wolf chasing an eagle, and because of the design, the eagle was chasing the wolf and so on. Calvin's tattoo was different. Calvin's tattoo was of a wolf chasing a *scarab* chasing the wolf.

"Cal, we need to talk," I said and for the second time today I passed out.

This time when I woke up Calvin was making something in the kitchen which gave me a moment to collect myself. I reached for my bag and starting looking for something. When Cal came in with a steaming mug, I handed him my dream diary in exchange.

"Hot cocoa," he said, "Are you feeling any better? I can make you something to eat if you're hungry."

"Thanks, I'm good. I think you should read that though. There's not much there, but it's only been happening for a few nights," I said.

He looked confused, but sat opposite me in the armchair and flipped open the notebook. I was blowing on the cocoa while covertly keeping an eye on Cal over the mug and watched his face blanch as he read.

"How much do you know?" he asked quietly.

"Not enough," I answered.

"Do you know? Do you know about me?" he asked.

"No. Not really. I think there were clues in the dreams, but we always ran out of time. I just have a feeling," I said hoping he'd explain what was going on.

"It's going to sound crazy," he said looking worried.

"Cal, this is me Yuki. I'm like the queen of crazy," I said. "I smell dead people. Remember?"

"O.k., but it's a long story. I think we're going to need more cocoa," he said getting up to put the kettle on the stove.

"Uh Cal? Is it a really long story?" I asked.

He looked back at me from the kitchen with one eyebrow raised.

"Could I take you up on that food after all?" I asked.

Then we both laughed. I came into the kitchen wrapped in his blanket and we joked like we always did. For the first time in days it was like nothing had changed. I had my friend back.

"Yuki," Calvin said as he came up beside me, "Can I kiss you?"

Well, maybe a few things had changed.

Chapter 20

*F*ollowing a monster sized bagel slathered in cream cheese and a dreamy kiss from Cal, I settled on the couch. We were sitting facing each other, each with our backs against an armrest, my short legs leaning against his longer ones. I knew that what Cal was about to say was important and had the potential to change things between us, but I felt strangely relaxed. *Ready.* I was about to learn the truth.

Calvin's face shifted between worried, excited, happy and scared. I reached for his hand to let him know I was here for him.

Looking from my hand to my face he smiled. "I guess I should start at the beginning," he said grinning ruefully. "I'm not like other guys," he said looking away.

No you're not Calvin Miller.

"But it's difficult to explain," he said squeezing my hand, "are you sure you want to know?" Cal looked up at me through his shaggy bangs and his blue eyes were questioning.

"Yes," I whispered. Just one word but it seemed to be enough.

Calvin sat up straighter and began. "I'm connected to the wolf that you saw in your dream. I know that sounds crazy, but it's true. You wrote in your dream journal that you saw a man and a wolf and a countryside ravaged by drought," he said. "Do you remember what it looked like?" he asked.

"It was horrible," I said closing my eyes for a moment. "There was so much pain there. It was like the land was crying but it was too dry for tears." Embarrassed I opened my eyes to see Calvin looking at me intently.

"What you saw in your dream was true," he said, "hundreds of years ago that place existed. There was a group of people and a pack of wolves that lived off the land in harmony. They weren't friends exactly, but they respected each other. Then came the drought that killed the plants and the trees and dried up the lakes and rivers. Animals began to die and the birds stopped their singing. The ground dried up and was carried away on the wind. After many months of drought the humans had depleted their food stores of berries and dried meats and the wolves had ranged far to find prey. It was then, beneath a full moon, that the leader of the humans and the alpha wolf met on the hill where they could look out and see the suffering of their people."

Cal cleared his throat and sipped from his mug of cocoa. One tear rolled down his cheek before he breathed deeply and began again. "The wolves of this place were old and pure. They were the great Silver Wolves who had long ago been touched by the Creator. These wolves had never left this place and so had not mixed with the other wolves of the world. Their blood still flowed with old magic. What the alpha wolf proposed that night was a pact. To save both of their peoples the wolves would give up their bodies so that the humans would continue to have children and survive. The humans in turn would carry the spirits of the wolves so that they would live on forever." Calvin closed his eyes as though trying to recall the story and whispered, "The humans did survive and the Silver Wolves live on inside their children. When a child descended from these people reaches maturity the wolf spirit within begins to awaken." Opening his eyes Cal looked at me sadly. "I am one of those people Yuki," he said in a small voice so unlike him, "I thought I was going crazy, but it's true. My dad finally told me. It follows his bloodline." "Yuki," he said, "I'm scared."

I sat there stunned. Calvin was still holding my hand and I wanted to reach out and hold him and tell him everything would be alright, but I sat there rooted to the couch. Questions were racing through my head and I had no idea what to ask first. Without meaning to I blurted out the one that kept dancing through my mind like crazy. "Does that make you a werewolf?" I asked, then wished I hadn't. It sounded silly when I said it out loud.

Calvin laughed, but he didn't sound happy. "That's kind of hard to answer," he said looking sullen. "If you're asking if I change into a wolf around the full moon, then I guess the answer is yes. I'm a werewolf," he said with disgust. "It's not like in the movies though," he said and shuddered. *You're a werewolf Calvin Miller.*

I suddenly wished that I hadn't had that bagel and all those cups of cocoa. I had kissed him. I had kissed a werewolf. Did that mean I was, like, infected? If we had kids would they be little furballs? *Yuki, get a grip, get a grip, get a grip.* First, ixnay on the furballsay. Calvin had been a normal kid, so obviously he wasn't born a baby wolf cub. Second, he had said the wolf spirit lived in the people of the old bloodline. It was a lot to process, but it seemed like I wasn't going to sprout claws or fur anytime soon. *No Yuki, you just get to smell dead people.*

Suddenly a thought occurred to me. "Cal, is that why you missed school and didn't come over this weekend?" I asked. I realized that I hadn't just seen a full moon in my dreams. The nights had been really bright all weekend.

"Yah, things have been weird for a while now, but my dad could tell that it was finally going to happen this time," he said, "so just before the full moon my parents brought me out into the woods. It's, um, easier there."

He looked embarrassed again and I wondered what it must have been like. Trying to think of something that would make him feel better I said, "He's beautiful you know. Your wolf." *You're beautiful Calvin Miller.*

I squeezed his hand and moved closer to him on the couch. "So you only change around the full moon, right?" I asked a mischievous smile playing on my lips.

"Yes," Cal answered, the blue of his eyes deepening.

"Good, then it's just the two of us," I said and kissed him.

I kissed a werewolf and I liked it.

Chapter 21

Cal had offered to give me a ride to school the next day, but I had already made plans with Emma. When Emma pulled up she couldn't wait to find out about my plant research. *Oh that.*

"Um, I kind of got distracted," I answered with a slow smile.

"Wait, did something happen with you and Calvin?" she asked.

"Uh, you could say that," I said turning to her in the driver's seat. "We kissed. It was awesome."

Emma squealed and congratulated me. "So do you think he'll go veggie now that the two of you are dating?" Emma asked.

I tried to picture a wolf eating tofu. *Not so much.* "No, probably not," I answered.

"Good. I need a victim to practice my arguments on," she said and we both laughed.

Things were good and life was going back to normal. Except my boyfriend was a werewolf and I smell dead people. *Almost normal.*

Calvin was waiting for me at my locker. He was leaning against the wall of lockers and looked good in his blue jeans and t-shirt that stretched tight across the chest. *Better than good.* My eyes slid over to his right arm and I made a mental note to ask him about his tattoo. I'd have to wait until after classes were over since we couldn't talk about his wolf issues here at school. We also hadn't decided if we should tell Emma. Telling your friend you turn into a wolf each month around the full moon was a bit more complicated than telling her you had a strange psychic ability. Shaking off stressful thoughts, I went to go spend a few minutes with my boyfriend before class.

At lunch time Emma and I filled Cal in on the details of our visit to the Green farm and our impressions of Grace Green. Emma went on about how Grace was a heinous violator of bee labor rights and I finally worked in the bit about me suspecting her of murder. Calvin was taking it well, but I could tell he was concerned.

"I don't think either of you should go back to that farm," he said looking back and forth between us, "just in case."

Emma looked like she was going to argue but then sighed. "I don't think I could face those poor subjugated bees," Emma said, "at least not until we find a way to overthrow the evil despot."

"Would putting her away for murder fall into that plan?" I asked innocently. Emma and I smiled wickedly at each other.

"That would do perfectly," Emma said.

Calvin just looked back and forth between us and threw up his hands. "I'm going to get another burger," he grumbled, "and leave the plans for world domination to you two."

He walked away to peals of laughter. When it came to planning world domination, or in this case how to bring down a murderer, I was glad to have Emma on my side. She was good at research and once she set herself a goal she never gave up.

I asked Calvin to give me a ride home and hang out after school and for Emma to come by after dinner. That way I would get a chance to ask Calvin about his tattoo and we could still fit in some ghost research. I was pleased to have a plan of action and my boots squeaked as I bounced all the way to my next class. *Don't worry Jackson, I'll help you find your way. I can be your flame in the darkness. I know I can.*

Chapter 22

Cal was waiting for me by his truck after school. He was leaning against it reading something as I approached. As he closed the notebook, I realized it was my dream diary. "Sorry, I forgot to give this back to you yesterday," he said handing the diary back to me.

"Thanks, there's actually something from my dreams that I still need to ask you about," I said as I stuffed the notebook into my backpack.

Calvin held out his hand and pulled me to him. "You can ask me anything," he said, "anything at all."

"It's about your tattoo," I said looking up at him.

"Oh," he said looking uncomfortable. "That's kind of hard to explain," he answered.

"More difficult than explaining about turning furry?" I asked playfully. "Because I find that hard to believe." I was trying for the one eyebrow raise, but was pretty sure that I was failing miserably.

"Can we take a detour on the way to your house?" Calvin asked. "It would be easier to talk about somewhere else," he said.

"Sure," I said and gave him a quick hug before getting into his truck.

Cal drove out towards his parent's house, but just before his driveway he turned onto a muddy dirt road. I realized that he was taking me out to his dad's workshop. I hadn't been out here for years, but I remembered the pottery wheel and the smell of clay from previous visits. His dad claimed that working with clay was therapeutic and helped to relieve stress. My few failed attempts didn't make me a believer, but I knew Cal always liked to hang out in the workshop as a kid.

Cal pulled his truck to a stop and we walked up to what looked like a small cabin. Calvin let us inside and I was surprised to see a small cot and desk had been added against one wall.

"Have you been living out here?" I asked. It wasn't far from his parent's house but the trees gave the cabin a feeling of privacy.

"Sort of. I needed some space when I was trying to understand the changes over the summer," Cal said, "and my dad seemed to understand. He let me use his workshop when I needed to get away and couldn't get out to one of our retreats in the woods."

In the woods. I realized that there was still a lot I had to learn about his wolf side.

"Here," Cal said handing me a folding chair. "It's not the Ritz, but we don't have to worry about people listening in," he said. "So you wanted to know more about my tattoo?" he asked.

"Yah, can I see it again?" I asked. Calvin pushed his t-shirt sleeve higher up his arm so that the tattoo showed clearly against his tanned skin. "Where did you get it done?" I asked reaching out but not quite touching it.

Cal saw my hesitation and moved his arm closer. "It's o.k. you can touch it if you want," he said. "I had it done by a friend of my father," he answered. "There is a tradition amongst the old blood that when a child reaches the age of change they are to be marked with the image of the wolf spirit that resides within them," he said starting to blush. "We are also marked with the symbol that grounds us. The second symbol usually represents our soul mate and comes to us in a vision, kind of like the symbols in your dreams." He was definitely blushing now.

You're blushing Calvin Miller.

It was then that I saw the second symbol, the thing that the wolf was chasing around Cal's arm and that in

70

turn was chasing the wolf. "Calvin is that a dung beetle?" I asked incredulously.

"Sacred scarab," he muttered.

I remembered the tattoo of the wolf and eagle on the arm of the man in my dream. His soul mate must have been represented by an eagle and Calvin's by a scarab.

"Is that supposed to represent me?" I asked. I wasn't sure if I should be happy about that or irritated.

"If I say yes, are you going to hit me?" he asked.

I looked from Calvin's face to his arm and back to his face again. Rolling my eyes I sighed, "I just don't like having a beetle for a spirit animal. I am glad you chose me though."

"It was fate," he said and kissed my forehead. "My dung beetle princess," he said with a grin.

I moved to hit him, but he was already running out the door to his truck. Laughing, I ran after him. *You better run Calvin Miller.*

Chapter 23

*W*e grabbed a drive-thru dinner. I ordered a salad and Calvin ordered three burgers and drove to my house. I had a bit of a mishap with the dressing packet and was wearing half of it on my shirt. I sulked that Cal must have driven over a bump, but it was probably just my bad luck catching up with me. Today had been fun and exciting. If the worst that happened was me having to smell like a condiment, I wasn't complaining. I could barely smell anything other than vinegar anyway. *I'm working on it Jackson.*

I left Calvin in the kitchen where he was finishing his last burger and ran upstairs to change my shirt. I tossed the soiled shirt into the laundry hamper and grabbed a tissue tee and cardigan. As I pulled my hair through the shirt collar to hang loose at my back I felt a prickling sensation along my arms and the hair rose at the back of my neck. I could have sworn I was being watched.

Making sure that Calvin hadn't followed me upstairs, I tiptoed back to the door and looked up and down the hallway. *Nobody there.* Crouching down I tiptoed across my bedroom to the window. Careful not to cast a silhouette I slid the curtain aside an inch and peered out. The sky was darkening, casting everything in the gray monochrome of twilight. A streetlight a few driveways down was beginning to flicker on, but that was the only movement I could see. I waited a few more seconds but didn't notice anything suspicious. *I guess it was nothing.* I slowly stood up and sighed, chiding myself for being jumpy, but as I went to leave the room I turned back and hung the bell covered ribbon across my windows. *Better safe than sorry.*

Twenty minutes later Emma was standing in my bedroom dangling papers in front of our faces and asking who the supreme goddess of research was.

"If I say it's you can I read those printouts?" I asked hopefully.

Calvin just rolled his eyes and reached for the papers.

"While you two lovebirds were off playing, I went to the library and did some hardcore research," Emma said smugly.

"Playing?" I asked, "How do you know we weren't doing research too?" We hadn't been, but she didn't know that.

Emma looked at my newly changed shirt, not the same one that I had been wearing at school today, and winked. I blushed so bad my face felt like it was on fire. A million excuses, all true, ran through my brain, but I realized that they would just incriminate me further.

Sighing I said, "Emma, supreme goddess of research, please illuminate us with your wisdom."

Emma nodded at me then put her hands on her hips and gazed imperiously down her nose at Calvin. They both stared at each other until Emma finally looked away first. *Did he just growl?* Before the two of them could get into some crazy battle for dominance, I grabbed a pillow and tossed it at Cal. Calvin grudgingly moved over to make room for Emma. Giggling, I asked Emma for the scoop. She finally sat on the bed and spilled about her trip to the library.

"In the media library I found where they had archived local newspapers going back to the date of the boating accident that killed all three of Jackson and Grace Green's sons," Emma said. "They had copies of articles from papers with such tiny circulations that they don't have websites," she explained.

What she had just said was sinking in. If these local papers weren't online, then I wouldn't have found their articles when I did my Internet search. It made sense since the only articles I found were from the larger newspapers based in Portland, Portsmouth, and Boston.

"I hit, I do believe, pay dirt," Emma said gloating. She was really loving this.

In the end Emma had proven to indeed be the supreme goddess of research. There was a journalist who seemed to have taken an interest in the case of the three brothers drowning and he wrote an article, and a later follow up article, on the events surrounding their deaths. Apparently the three brothers had come to Maine to vacation at their parent's farm, however, their father had been too busy with his business to go off fishing with them. Jackson Green was lobbying against the use of airborne pesticides, which he felt threatened his organic farm, and spent the day at the Statehouse in Augusta. The three brothers borrowed their father's boat and went out fishing on a nearby lake. When they didn't return home for dinner their mother, Grace Green, called the police and fire department. It was over twelve hours before state forest rangers trained as emergency divers could make it to the scene. By then all three men were confirmed dead by accidental drowning. Later investigation showed that poor upkeep of the Green's boat had likely led to the boating accident.

"The thing is," Emma was saying, "Grace Green never seemed to forgive her husband for the death of her sons. She blamed his devotion to his business for their deaths, since he had both neglected repairs on the family boat and hadn't gone with their sons that day."

Son of a dung beetle.

"When you add her grief and her anger at her husband to the poisonous plant *Deadly Nightshade* we found growing in her herb garden, it does sound suspicious," I said. The words barely left my mouth before I was smothered in vinegar. The smell was so intense I felt like I was suffocating. I reached for my throat trying to breathe and little flashes of light started to spot my vision. I guess we were onto something. *Please, oh please, make it stop.*

Chapter 24

*W*ith a wash of wet dog smell, the vinegar smell faded and I could breathe freely again.

"Yuki, are you o.k.?" Calvin asked placing his arm around my shoulders. "Do you need to lie down?" he asked. He sounded worried. Had his wolf spirit somehow protected me?

"I'm better now, thanks," I said taking another deep breath. "I think Jackson was trying to let us know that our suspicions were correct," I said looking at Cal and Emma, "I just wasn't ready for the vinegar assault."

Calvin was the first to ask what we were probably all thinking, "So what do we do now?"

Good question.

"I think Jackson would want his contributions to go to the charities that he had set aside money for," I said hoping our discussion wouldn't trigger another violent smell impression. The smell became stronger but not too strong. Maybe Cal's wolf spirit was providing a barrier. *Thank you.* "I think that was a smell signal for yes," I added.

"What about Grace Green's inheritance?" Emma asked, "Would he want his money going to a murderer?" It was a good question.

"We could send everything to the police with a copy of the articles you found and copies of the pictures from the garden," Cal suggested. "If we include an anonymous letter with our suspicions they would have to investigate."

They both looked expectantly at me.

"This is going to sound crazy, but I think I have an idea," I said feeling a little silly that I hadn't tried this before.

I grabbed a notebook and flipped it open to a clean page. I then grabbed a black sharpie marker and wrote in large letters the words "YES," "MAYBE," and "NO." Emma and Calvin both looked at the page confused.

"It's like a Ouija board," I explained, "except Jackson won't be pushing a pointer to the answer. We'll ask a question that he should feel strongly about and see if his smell impression gets stronger on one of the answers."

Calvin reached for my hand and squeezed it once. "Are you sure you're ready for that?" he asked, "It sounds like it could get intense. Jackson's ghost almost overwhelmed you earlier."

I wished there was some way to communicate my suspicion about his wolf spirit helping me. Emma was sitting there watching us both and listening intently though, so there was no way to talk to him about it.

"I think I can do it with you here," I said a little breathlessly.

He was leaning in close now and my heart was starting to beat faster. "O.k.," he said and squeezed my hand.

Emma rolled her eyes. "Can we get this show on the road?" she asked, "No offense Yuki, but I have a date with a mud mask tonight. Some of us still need to find a date for the homecoming dance."

I closed my eyes concentrating on the question. "Jackson, do you want us to go to the police?" I asked. With a shaking hand I pointed at YES, then MAYBE. On maybe the smell impression was strong. "I think that's a maybe," I said.

"Can we ask if he wants his wife arrested?" Emma asked hopefully.

"O.k. Do you want your wife Grace arrested for your murder?" I asked. I pointed to YES, there was no smell, then MAYBE and NO. On no I felt dizzy and the room flooded with the smell of vinegar. I could still breathe, but the smell was incredibly strong. "That's a no," I gasped. Panting a little I looked up to see Calvin shake his head.

"That's it for tonight Yuki," he said firmly, "we can finish this tomorrow."

I wanted to argue, but he was right. I was completely worn out and a headache was creeping up from my temples.

"Emma, it looks like you'll have time for your mud mask after all," I sighed, trying to smile.

Emma helped pick the papers up off the bed, laying them on the nightstand and Calvin told her he'd make sure I got some rest.

"Night then Yuki," she said on her way out, "don't ever let anyone tell you your life is dull." Turning to Calvin she said, "Take good care of her."

When the front door closed, Calvin came over and started unlacing my boots. I could barely keep my eyes open.

"Calvin Miller did you slip me a roofie because I feel like I'm about to pass out," I mumbled.

Cal laughed and pulled the blankets up under my chin. He came back a minute later with a glass of water. "Drink up, Dung Beetle Princess," he said handing me the glass. "Working with spirit will drain you fast, especially when you're just learning how to use it," he said. Setting the glass over on the nightstand, he stood to leave. "Goodnight Yuki," he said and leaned down to kiss my forehead. He ran his finger along my cheek brushing hair off my face.

Goodnight Calvin. I was sucked down into the dark oblivion of dreamless sleep.

Chapter 25

I woke up to a pounding headache and the acrid smell of vinegar burning my nose. *Go suck eggs Jackson,* I thought as I rolled over and pressed the snooze button on my alarm clock. *Go suck pickled eggs Vinegar Dude.* Calvin was right. I needed to be more careful when dealing with the spirits of the dead. What I needed now was knowledge. Was there someone out there who could teach me how to control my power? I couldn't face the thought of feeling this horrible for the rest of my life. There had to be an easier way.

I made a mental note to ask Calvin about his training. He had made it sound like he was learning to work with his wolf spirit, but hadn't elaborated. Once classes were over today, I was going to drill him for details. For a moment I wished that Emma was privy to Calvin's new werewolf status. Emma was an awesome interrogator. *That girl could get a block of tofu to talk.* Laughing at the thought of squealing tofu, I opened my eyes and faced the day.

The school day seemed to drag on forever. The halls were buzzing with excitement about the homecoming dance. Streamers in school colors were hung above lockers and around doorways. I was already on sensory overload and the inescapable bright colors and hum of conversation were making my headache worse.

"If you keep frowning like that, you're going to stick that way" Emma said at lunchtime.

I winced as someone dropped their lunch tray. The clatter of silverware hitting the painted concrete floor was like someone sending icy spikes through my brain.

"Oh, that face is even worse," Emma said dramatically, "go back to the first expression quick. If you keep wincing like that, I'm going to lose my appetite."

"Emma, you never have an appetite," I said feeling a little grouchy.

"I have an excellent appetite but how am I supposed to eat while surrounded by the smell of death?" Emma asked.

"Hey, isn't that my line?" I joked.

"No, you smell ghosts but I smell death. Every time someone sits at our table with a burger or pepperoni pizza I feel like I'm trying to eat my lunch at an autopsy table," she said and shuddered. "It's totally disgusting," she added.

I looked down at my yogurt and suddenly didn't feel so hungry. With a warning twist from my stomach, I pushed the yogurt cup a foot away.

"See. Who's having appetite issues now?" Emma asked archly.

Emma was a great person to have around if you needed to go on a diet.

"So, you need a ride home today?" Emma asked.

I figured that was her way of asking if things were still going well between me and Calvin. "No thanks. Calvin is driving me home later," I said, a smile crossing my face.

"I thought so," Emma said, "He seemed really worried when you went all spacey last night. I figured things were getting serious between you two."

Were we getting serious? I didn't have enough experience in the dating department to know. "We're not getting married anytime soon if that's what you mean," I joked. I had intended to sound lighthearted but I stumbled a bit on the M word.

"Whose getting married?" Calvin asked as he sat down next to me.

I hadn't heard him come up behind me and I started to blush. Emma winked at me then laughed. *Thanks for the heads up Emma.*

Chapter 26

Calvin and I went back to his dad's workshop cabin after school. It was peaceful here without the watchful eyes and prying ears we had to deal with in the school hallways.

Earlier today I had overheard a sophomore telling a group of freshman that the school witch had cursed one of the hot senior boys into going out with her. I was nearly to my next class when I realized they had been gossiping about me and Calvin. If they were going to talk about me, and claim that I could cast spells on boys, I wished that they at least had the decency to call me Yuki the Enchantress or something. I guess I was still stuck with witch. I never should have bought that evil eye pendant. How much luck had it brought me? *Zero, zip, nada.*

Calvin came back into the cabin with blankets he had brought over from the main house. *Well, maybe that pendant had brought me a little luck.* He was dressed all in black today and it made his eyes look like dark pools of water. I could drown in those eyes.

"Sorry it's so drafty," Cal apologized.

We both wrapped ourselves in clean smelling blankets and curled up on two armchairs facing each other. The armchairs looked worn, but they hadn't been here on my last visit. I wondered fleetingly if Calvin had stolen them from his parent's family room. They looked vaguely familiar. *His parents must really be worried about him.*

"I'd like you to go camping with me in a few weeks," Calvin said surprising me, "when we get closer to the new moon."

My thoughts were immediately swept up in daydreams of being alone with Cal in the woods. *In a tent.* I had never been a big fan of camping in the great buggy outdoors, but if it meant a weekend alone with Cal I was game. Then a question struck me. "Why the new moon?" I asked.

"They almost always have Wolf Camp as far away from the full moon as possible," he said, "for obvious reasons. It's hard to learn focus when you're shifting into a wolf." Calvin smiled his toothy grin.

"Wolf Camp?" I asked incredulously.

"Well, that's what some of us call it," he said, "I don't think it really has a name."

"Would they even let me come with you?" I asked, "Since, you know, I'm not a wolf."

Just dating one.

"They'll make a special exception for you," he said, "since you're touched by spirit. We have teachers who can help you learn to control your powers and communicate with my wolf. Well, at least that's what my dad says."

Cal had been talking about me to his dad? This was getting weirder by the second.

"What kind of camp is this?" I asked.

What was I getting myself into? I didn't think I wanted to be the only vanilla human alone in the woods with a camp filled with wolf possessed nature enthusiasts.

"It's a lot like a corporate team building retreat," Calvin said and laughed. "We do team building and trust exercises," he said, "but we also work on meditation and how to focus our will. We learn how to communicate with our wolf spirit and ways to gain more control over our change. They even have couples therapy."

"They offer couples therapy?" I asked, surprised, "Is that why they let other humans come to camp?"

Calvin looked embarrassed. "Well, not exactly. Most of our kind mate, um I mean hook up, with other wolves," he said. "One of the elders said that our blood sings to one another."

Great. *Howling blood.*

"But I'm not a wolf," I said stating the obvious.

"That's because I'm one of the Chosen Ones," Cal said looking embarrassed again. "The others look for wolf partners, but each generation a child is gifted with the spirit of the original alpha wolf. When this child reaches adulthood, he will hear the singing of one touched by spirit, but not by wolf."

Like me.

"Does that mean that the others all have tattoos of two wolves chasing each other around their arms?" I asked. I knew that I had more important questions, but for the moment I couldn't think of one.

"Yah, they have two wolves and alphas like me have a different second symbol," he said. "So in a way we're marked. We are the destined leaders of our people, so it's another way for people to know that I am the alpha when in human form, though most of us can sense it."

I suddenly noticed the worry lines around his eyes. Calvin was taking this all pretty seriously and he must have already been feeling the weight of responsibility. Responsibility for a role he hadn't chosen, but had been born into.

"So my being touched by spirit, but not by wolf, is a good thing?" I asked.

I was still curious about how the alphas were different. I remembered the man in my dream having a tattoo of a wolf chasing an eagle. He must have carried the alpha wolf spirit too.

"A very good thing," Calvin said closing the space between us. "You are the anchor that keeps me from losing touch with my human self," he said while his breath brushed my cheek, "and the crazy thing is that my wolf spirit is *your* anchor."

I was about to tell him that he *was* crazy when I remembered the wolf, his wolf, holding my shirt in its teeth to keep me from following the butterflies into the light. Maybe it wasn't so far-fetched after all.

"So it's fate then?" I asked with him so close my lips brushed the line of his jaw with each word, "Us being together?"

"Absolutely," Calvin said with a low growl. Then he lifted my chin, tilting my head back, and kissed me deeply.

Who was I to argue with Fate?

Chapter 27

I was getting excited for Wolf Camp. Who would have thought I'd ever get excited for camping? The more Calvin and I talked about camp, the more animated he became and his enthusiasm was contagious. I printed a lunar calendar from a website I found about moon phases and taped it on the wall beside my bed. Each morning I would wake up and mark off another day with a big red X. I was happy to be moving away from the full moon and towards a fun weekend with my boyfriend.

Calvin was also a bit worried. Last night he had confided his concern about the moon phases. Since his wolf spirit was growing weaker the further we moved away from the full moon, he worried that it may become too weak to protect me. It made me hesitate to use my powers before learning more from the teachers at camp. So I tried to be patient and ignore the vinegar presence of Jackson Green's ghost. I had promised Cal that I wouldn't use my makeshift Ouija board without him here with me and I intended to keep that promise.

I was doing well in school so far this semester which was a pleasant surprise for my parents. They thought that Calvin was a good influence on me. Cal and I got together for after school study sessions every day, but we didn't do a lot of studying in the traditional sense. I probably had Emma to thank for the increase in my GPA. She was helping me find my way around the library since my new enthusiasm in research. If I couldn't work on my spirit skills, then I could at least brush up on some basic investigative methods.

I was also starting to think about college. Would Calvin be able to attend college next year if his shapeshifting became more intense? If so, could we get into the same school? I hadn't worried about the future all that much before, but suddenly I had so much to plan for. It was a little overwhelming.

Most of the time I just tried to focus on the task at hand. I studied hard, tried to work on my yoga breathing, planned for the upcoming camping trip, and every once in awhile I would practice for the homecoming dance by twirling around my room in the corset dress I still hadn't had a chance to wear in public. *Soon my lovely, soon.*

Chapter 28

I marked a red X on my lunar calendar with a smile. *Today was the day*. I was going with Cal to Wolf Camp. I was vacillating between nervous and ecstatic. Going through the outfits that I had packed, I would wonder if something was appropriate for camp and my hands would start to shake. *Nervous*. Grabbing my dream diary, I remembered Calvin kissing me the last time we were distracted while reading it. *Ecstatic*. I was wound so tight that if I did snap I was going to fly out into the stratosphere. I really needed to work on my calming skills.

Zipping up my backpack, I glanced one more time in the mirror. The face staring back at me looked haunted. *Well you are being haunted Yuki*. My pale skin looked nearly translucent and the dark circles around my eyes hadn't been applied with makeup. Though I hadn't reached out to Jackson Green's spirit for answers, I was still easily fatigued. I continued to be visited by strange symbolic images in my dreams which left me tired and dizzy feeling. Having my sleep interrupted also, apparently, left me with a deathly pallor. I nearly looked like a ghost myself. *O.k. Casper let's go camping*.

The drive to the camping area took about four hours, but I didn't mind since I was riding with Calvin. The sun was high in the sky when we pulled onto the dirt road leading to the parking area. It was then another thirty minutes of hiking to our rendezvous point.

My earlier excitement was waning as my boots caught at every root and rock and my hair snagged on endless clawing tree branches. Cal seemed to know intuitively where to best place his feet on the overgrown trail. Leave it to Calvin to make this look easy. He always seemed in his element when doing something active outdoors which I guess made sense considering his wolf spirit. He looked back with his eyebrow raised when he realized I had lagged so far behind. *Rub it in wolf boy.*

"We're nearly there, but we can stop if you need to rest," he said looking perfectly well rested himself.

Calvin wasn't sweaty and didn't have one speck of dirt on him. I felt another bead of sweat trickle down my back to meet all of its friends where my pack pressed against my waist. I was sure that when I finally removed my backpack there was going to be large wet marks all over my shirt. *Gross.*

"Remind me never to do this again," I said pausing for a moment to catch my breath.

Calvin passed me a bottle of water. I cracked the seal on the cap and gulped down most of its contents.

"Ready?" he asked.

"Sure. I'm just a glutton for punishment," I muttered and we set off again.

Cal had been right. We only had to walk another ten minutes to reach camp. We pushed through a thick screen of hemlock trees that were growing close to the ground and burst out into a clearing.

So this is Wolf Camp. It wasn't exactly what I had pictured, though I'm not really sure what I had expected. *More teeth and claws?* I surveyed the faces of the camp residents who all seemed too busy to mind my stares. In fact they all appeared to be doing something industrious. There were no young children that I could see. The older men and women were cooking, building, or playing instruments. The majority of the people here though were in their teens and twenties. They tended to either fall into the group working silently on art projects or the more rowdy group playing team sports or hacky sack. In fact, there were tons of them playing what looked like synchronized hacking. It was mind boggling and yet beautiful. I wondered if they could teach me and immediately regretted wearing a skirt.

Cal followed my gaze to the kids playing hack and smiled. "Come on," he said reaching out to take my hand, "there are some friends I'd like you to meet."

With a nod and a growing tightness in my chest I walked with Calvin to be introduced to his extended wolfy family.

The guys and girls playing hacky sack were hard to classify. There were lots of long, white girl dreads and beaded hemp bracelets that made me think crunchy hippie chicks and loads of tanned guys with sun bleached hair and a rolling way of walking that made me think surfer dudes, but really that was an over-generalization. The common thread here seemed to be their love of the outdoors and a feeling in my gut that they all genuinely liked each other. Was it their shared wolf spirits? I really didn't know, but I suddenly felt a pang of jealousy for what they all shared with Calvin and with each other. *Harmony.* They all moved and reacted to one another with an innate harmony. Maybe their blood is singing out to one another like how Calvin had said their blood calls for their mates. I quickly tried to banish the thought. It wasn't helping my sudden feeling of jealousy. *Since when did I get jealous?*

My jealous worries disappeared the moment Calvin introduced me. He put his arm around me with obvious pride and affection and the open smiling faces were so welcoming that I felt like a heel for my earlier reaction.

"Hey Yuki, you want to play?" one of the girls asked.

I suddenly really, really wanted to. "Sure! But um, do you ever play in a hack circle?" I asked. I wasn't sure how to do the synchronized form of the game. I had never even seen it before coming here. *Probably a wolf thing.*

In answer the girl ran up and hugged me then stepped back and exclaimed, "Sure thing."

It was all a little overwhelming. Was I accepted as part of the group, or rather part of the pack, that simply?

If so, this wolf stuff was pretty awesome. With a huge silly grin on my face I looked over to see if Calvin was going to play too.

He pulled his t-shirt up over his head and tossed it to the ground. "Game on," Calvin announced with his toothy grin.

Oh yah, he was the alpha. Every kid in the area, even the ones who had previously been working sedately on art projects, raced over to us and formed a circle. Not worried anymore about fitting in, I tied the loose edges of my skirt up so they wouldn't trip me or catch on the hack. *Right, game on.*

I was a bit sad to leave the others since they had all been so friendly, but we promised to hang with all of them tomorrow. We set off for the other side of camp towards a medium sized tent set apart from the others. I was about to meet Cal's wolf spirit guru and my sense of ease was evaporating to be replaced by nervous anticipation. What kind of guy would Calvin have for a teacher? I realized that there was so much about Cal's other life that I just didn't know about yet.

Chapter 29

Simon was fascinating. He had sapphire blue eyes with smile lines at the creases, ruddy skin, dark stubble, and dark hair that always looked like he had just run his fingers though it leaving it sticking up in all directions. He was in a word, hot. *Well, for an older guy.* Simon also had a dramatic distinguishing feature, a pale scar that bisected his right ear and ran down his otherwise tan cheek terminating at the corner of his lip.

Noticing the direction of my gaze Simon quipped, "Makes me devastatingly handsome to the ladies."

I met his eyes and blushed.

"They say it gives me a roguish appeal," he said in his deep gravelly voice.

Calvin rolled his eyes and I could tell from his expression that he had heard this line many times before.

"We better go on in before Simon starts drooling over himself," Calvin teased. He held the flap of Simon's tent open for me and I ducked my head to enter.

Once inside, the tent was large and roomy with plenty of room to stand. Calvin followed me in with Simon entering last. Before Simon closed the tent flap he said something to someone outside who then moved to sit by the opening.

"We won't be disturbed now," Simon said with a wink.

I looked over at Cal but he just shrugged. Simon was behaving like the biggest flirt on the planet, but if it didn't bother Calvin then I wouldn't let it trouble me either.

Cal and I sat lotus style with our legs crossed, though it admittedly wasn't the most comfortable position in my boots. Simon readied a few things around the tent then sat across from us. He closed his eyes and when he looked at us again it was as though a completely different person sat across from us. *Now that's not creepy or anything.* I shivered involuntarily and Cal gripped my hand with a reassuring squeeze. Simon cocked his head to the side as though listening for something, all the while looking at me intently, and then he sniffed the air around me. *He was sniffing me?* Apparently satisfied with what he sensed, Simon then closed his eyes. When he opened them again a moment later he was back to his annoyingly charming self.

"Simon is very in tune with his wolf spirit," Calvin said, filling me in on the strange behavior. "He can let his wolf come to the surface, and yet retain his own form and sense of self, even now so far from the full moon." I realized that Cal's voice held a touch of awe.

"Aye love, my wolf came out to play," Simon said smiling his lopsided grin, "He says hello by the way." Simon said the last with another wink.

This was all too weird. Here I was sitting with Calvin and his playboy mentor and I was getting more confused by the second. I was wishing I had stayed outside with the kids my own age.

"You can lay off the theatrics Simon," Calvin said somewhat protectively.

He obviously respected his teacher but Simon's manner towards me was beginning to cross a line and I so did not want to be around to watch these two fight it out.

"So uh, how did you learn to do that?" I asked hoping to avoid any death and destruction on this camping trip.

It was the right thing to ask. Simon suddenly seemed to mellow and Cal relaxed.

"That's why you're here little scarab," Simon said. "I have been teaching Calvin how to communicate with his wolf and now I will try to help you as well."

Simon was much easier to deal with in teacher mode. I wondered how he could have so much wisdom, since he wasn't really all that old. He looked like he was probably in his late thirties or early forties.

As though reading my thoughts, Cal said, "Simon is unusual among our kind. He was born with full awareness of his wolf spirit. Because of this he learned to communicate with his wolf at a very young age and carries more wisdom than most of our elders."

It did explain a lot. There was something slightly off about Simon. It was hard to put a finger on, but being born possessed by a wolf spirit could make anyone a bit unhinged.

Simon smiled his lopsided grin and slapped Cal on the leg. "Don't go giving all my secrets away to the ladies. I need to hold something back to impress them with later." Wait for it. Simon winked at me, *again*.

I was hoping that we would get on with the teaching because my patience was running out. If Simon wasn't going to share his knowledge, then I was leaving and he could go pretend to be some other poor girl's dream beast. I was about to leave when Simon laughed.

"This one needs to learn patience," he said looking over at Calvin, "or the spirits of the dead will consume her. If she rushes into things, she might as well run into the light now and get it over with."

I wasn't sure if Simon was attempting to goad Calvin or reprimand me. He was doing a good job of both. Cal let a low growl rumble in the back of his throat but he didn't move. I settled back on the ground and tried to use my yoga breathing to calm down. *Think happy thoughts, think happy thoughts, think happy thoughts.* Maybe Simon was right. I was acting reckless and my calming attempts weren't really working. *I still wanted to slap him.* It was then that it occurred to me that he may have planned this from the start. Was this all an act to provoke me into losing my cool? *You won't break me that easily old man.*

Chapter 30

The rest of Wolf Camp was a blur of mental exercises with Simon, physical exercise with the other wolf kids, art therapy to help recapture elusive dream messages, and rare moments alone with Cal. I was learning so much information that my head was spinning, though that may also have been from lack of food. These people didn't seem to eat vegetables and I hadn't thought to bring my own provisions. After the first day of eating ketchup and mustard on otherwise empty burger buns, I decided to go on a fasting diet. Simon had mentioned that sometimes fasting would help to clear the mind and open oneself to communing with spirit. After half a day of drinking only water, I was beginning to think it was another one of his ways to torture me into losing my temper. I suspected that the only communing with spirit that actually took place was inside someone's food deprived hallucination.

I was beginning to consider making a break for it when Calvin came up behind me with an armload of fruit. He had apples, a pear, and a few green bananas, but to me he might as well have been carrying bars of gold.

"You're a god!" I exclaimed as he tossed me one of the apples.

"Thought you might like something other than bread and condiments," he chuckled.

"Hey, don't knock the condiments," I said and laughed. "Where did you score all of this?" I asked wondering if there was some secret hidden supermarket in the woods.

"I scavenged it off some of the older folks," Calvin replied. Then he laughed. "I traded them for some steaks

I brought with me," Cal said. "Sorry, I didn't think to bring all this myself."

I was too busy eating my second apple to reply, so I nodded instead. *All is forgiven.*

"We'll be heading back late tonight, so I told Simon he could have you for a few more hours." Looking at my sudden frown Cal added, "Sorry."

I knew Simon was trying to teach me how to control my powers, and how to call on Cal's wolf spirit for protection, but his teaching style left a lot to be desired.

"I know Simon can be a huge pain, but he's actually worried about you," Calvin said.

Worried about me? *Since when?* This was news to me and I stopped crunching on my apple so I wouldn't miss anything.

"Simon and I were working on my attempts to talk to my wolf spirit again, but I'm still having trouble. It's so alien, you know?" Cal said.

Yah, I did know. It was hard too. *Really, really hard.*

"Well, Simon got really frustrated because he said that one of us needs to learn this quick before Samhain," Cal said looking scared.

Samhain? Did he mean Halloween?

"Simon said that we need to try harder or we won't be prepared," Calvin was looking really distressed now. "He said that since your powers awakened you have only had to deal with one, maybe two, ghosts haunting you at a time. But on certain nights of the year the world is flooded with ghosts," Cal said.

He wasn't the only one becoming freaked out. I knew that I had a lot to learn about spirits, and my power to sense them, but I had never considered having to face multiple ghosts at once. It was a terrifying thought. I set my apple down no longer feeling hungry.

"Cal, this sounds bad. Really, really bad," I said.

"Yah, Simon is insistent that you focus on your training. He says that the next time the veil between worlds thins will be on Samhain," Calvin said, "which only gives us a little over a month to prepare."

It wasn't enough time. How could we possibly be ready in one month?

"Can the others help?" I asked. I tried to picture all the people in the camp lending their wolf spirits to fight off the spirits of the dead. It might work.

"No," Cal choked out, "They aren't bonded to you like I am. The only one with enough control to lend his wolf to the fight is Simon."

Great, I was going to be protected by a wolf spirit that neither Calvin nor I could yet speak to and the wolf spirit of a flirty psycho dude. *I was so dead.*

"You're panicking aren't you?" Cal asked.

"What? Me panic?" I asked trying for levity, "No way, not me." I didn't sound convincing.

"I'm sorry. I wasn't sure if I should tell you or not," Cal said. "I was afraid that telling you would make you worry, but that not telling you would mean you'd be unprepared."

I was standing here on a road with no roadmap. Or maybe it was with a map and no road. Either way I felt lost.

"I won't let anything bad happen to you," Calvin said, "We're in this together."

Together. The word gave me strength and as Cal reached out and held me in his arms I held out hope that we could keep each other safe. *Go team.*

Chapter 31

*A*greeing to give up my weekends to train with Calvin and Simon was easy, but getting my parent's consent was another thing. I couldn't exactly explain that thousands of ghosts, hungry for a haunting, were going to come drive me insane next month. There was no way that I could just casually drop the bomb at the dinner table saying, "Hey Mom and Dad, I smell dead people." I was so not ready for the big reveal. With my luck my parents would have me locked away in a psych ward, where the spirits of the dead could come terrorize me in a locked room. No. I couldn't tell my parents the truth, so we had to come up with a believable lie.

We created a new identity for Simon that would garner my parent's trust and a reason for us to be hanging out with him. Calvin claimed that Simon was his uncle who was staying at his parent's house temporarily. We fibbed that Simon was fixing up his camp, but that it needed to be winterized before he could move in. I added that Simon was having marital troubles, which was why he had moved here out of the blue. It was worth adding that tidbit to see the look of horror on Simon's face. He covered it well, but I don't think he'll ever forgive me for telling my parents that he had been married. *Oh the horror*.

In the end they finally agreed. I think Calvin was the deciding factor. My mom adored him and didn't seem to think him capable of a lie. Simon was also very believable as a sudden bachelor on the ropes. His five o'clock shadow at all hours of the day and night and his roguish personality lent credence to our story.

101

"That poor woman," my mom said one day, "I can't imagine anyone being married to that man."

I had to bite my lip to stifle a laugh.

Chapter 32

Returning to school also held its challenges. Emma wanted to know all about my weekend with Cal, but I had to censor everything relating to his wolf spirit which made conversation difficult. I could tell that Emma thought I was holding back. Hopefully she just thought I was shy about sharing details about me and Calvin.

"So did you two get cozy while camping?" Emma asked trying again for details.

It was the end of the school day and I had managed to avoid most of her questions at lunch by pointing out the new flyers for the homecoming dance. So much for keeping her distracted.

"Did you two share a tent?" Emma asked eagerly.

"No, we did not share a tent," I answered, "though we did kiss a few times."

"Yuki, what were you thinking? You should have shared a tent with Calvin. This was your big chance to bring out his protective side. You two could have cuddled together while he protected you from the scary monsters outside the tent," Emma insisted.

Protect me from scary monsters *outside* the tent? She really had no idea.

"Maybe next time," I said noncommittally while shrugging my shoulders. "It's not like the only time we'll ever go to Wo... Woods Camp," I stuttered. *Crap*. That was close. I was going to have to be more careful around Emma. I nearly let the wolf out of the bag.

"Well, are you guys going to try that séance thing again?" Emma asked, "I could come over after school today." She looked hopeful but I quickly dashed the idea.

"Sorry, I'm still having those headaches," I answered lamely, "and I promised Cal I wouldn't try the Ouija board again until I was at full strength."

"Oh hon, I didn't know you were still having those," Emma said, "I have a really good recipe for headache ease tea." Emma grabbed her books from her locker, looking thoughtful. "It tastes horrible," she admitted, "but it really works. I'll bring some over after dinner tonight."

Right then the last bell rang and we started to head towards the parking lot exit.

"Promise to drink it if I brew some up?" Emma asked.

"O.k. but it better not taste like that Echinacea tincture you made me try last month," I said with a shudder, "that stuff was pure evil."

At the time, Emma had told me to drink the Echinacea tincture to avoid coming down with an end of the summer cold. *I'd rather get sick.*

"You're right. That one left me feeling like I had fur on my tongue," Emma admitted. "Which would be a shame if you and Calvin were kissing." She said the last with a wink and headed to her car.

I was so not looking forward to drinking her tea. I was beginning to rethink sharing our wolf secret with Emma. I felt bad keeping something from my best friend. Calvin was having trouble keeping the truth from Emma as well. Neither one of us was good at telling lies. It would be easier if we didn't have to sneak around behind her back. *Plus, then I wouldn't have to drink her tea.*

Chapter 33

*A*t the end of the school week, Calvin and I drove to his dad's workshop where we had planned to meet Simon. Calvin had been working with Simon every day after school, but I hadn't seen Simon since Wolf Camp. I was nervous about seeing him again. There was something about Simon that made me uncomfortable. He was just so wild around the edges. I had witnessed some wolfish behavior around some of the others at camp, but with Simon I always felt like his wolf spirit was waiting just below the surface. More than once I glanced at Simon from the corner of my eye and could have sworn I saw a huge silver wolf over his shoulder. When I would try to look directly at it, the wolf would disappear. I never knew for sure if it was just my imagination, but it made me feel like someone else was in the room with us, watching me. It kind of gave me the creeps.

I drew strength from Calvin, and holding hands, we entered the cabin. It hadn't changed much since I had last visited. Simon obviously didn't have plans on staying here once our training was finished. *Fine by me.*

Simon, not getting up, waved us to sit. "Ah, my favorite spirit touched girl," Simon said with a flourish, "come to bring the light into the darkness of my day."

He was trying to be charming, but Simon's words struck too close to what I had been told about my duty to help lost souls find light in the darkness. I immediately thought of Jackson's ghost no doubt hovering nearby. *I will help you find the river of light Jackson. I promise.*

"Can I offer you the last bite?" Simon asked.

I looked down to realize he had been eating when we arrived. Exactly *what* he was eating I didn't want to know. Whatever he was eating, it was bloody and therefore very, very disgusting. Simon knew I was a vegetarian, so I had to wonder if this was just another one of his tests. He seemed to enjoy making me uncomfortable.

"Which one of you is eating that anyway, you or your wolf?" I asked.

I hadn't meant to sound so bold and I realized belatedly that it was actually a pretty rude thing to ask. Simon didn't look bothered by the question. *He was probably expecting it and I walked right into his trap.* I was beginning to get a headache. Verbal sparring with Simon always seemed to give me a headache. I might have to drink Emma's headache ease tea again. *No, not that. Anything but that.*

Eating that last bite of meat, Simon licked his bloody lips. He hesitated at the edge of his mouth where the corner of his lip was bisected by his scar. Then he slowly licked the shiny skin and smiled at me. The act was both sensual and disgusting. Leave it to Simon to find another reason for me to never eat meat. I felt my stomach churn and hoped I wouldn't give him the satisfaction of being sick. *Deep breaths Yuki.*

Setting his dish aside, Simon rested his elbows on the table and became very still, as though he was paying attention to something that only he could hear.

"Calvin's wolf spirit says that you are most open in your dreams, but he hasn't been able to contact you in the waking world," Simon said.

I nodded wondering what else Cal's wolf spirit was telling him.

"He also says that in time he will become your shield and Calvin will be the sword that you wield against the darkness," Simon said. "Together, you will be the flame to lead the lost souls to the light. But first you must listen to your teacher." I wondered if Simon added that last bit himself.

"What do I need to do?" I asked. I hadn't pictured myself as a warrior before, but the image was definitely cool. *Scary but cool.*

"First you must become one with the land. You must learn to reach out and feel the earth and nurture its children," Simon said grandly.

That sounded very cool.

"Your first lesson begins with these," Simon said, and handed me a packet of seeds.

I looked back at him blankly. "Seeds?" I managed to ask. I was totally confused.

"Come this way," Simon said, standing and walking to the door.

Calvin and I followed him outside behind the cabin. I looked over at Cal, but he looked just as confused as I did. *What was I getting myself into?*

Chapter 34

"Here is your first task," Simon said, "to work the land and nurture the life of the seeds in your hand." Simon waved his hand over a brown patch of dirt behind the cabin.

He wanted me to plant a garden? *He had to be kidding.*

Grabbing a trowel from a bucket full of gardening tools, Cal stepped forward. "I'll help you Yuki," he said.

"No Calvin, you will not," said Simon looking deadly serious. "This is part of Yuki's training and so for today she will work the land by herself."

I still had no idea what he was trying to do. "Uh, Simon could you maybe clarify what I'm supposed to be doing here?" I asked.

Simon met my eyes and it was all I could do not to flinch.

"You are going to till this soil and plant those seeds with your bare hands," Simon ordered.

My bare hands? This just keeps getting worse.

"While you do this, you are going to reach out and listen to the land and if you are lucky the land will tell you her secrets," Simon said. "Learn to listen to the land and you will be one step closer to listening to Calvin's wolf spirit," Simon added, "and to hearing the call of your spirit guide."

My spirit guide?

"Do you mean my spirit animal?" I asked. I was really confused now.

"Your animal totem will be your guide," Simon said, "listen to her wisdom if you wish to survive Samhain, when the dead walk the earth."

I shivered. So I was going to get dirty and hope my spirit animal would send me some kind of sign? I wasn't feeling very confident about Samhain. I looked to Calvin but he just shrugged.

"Sorry Yuki, I'll be back at the main house if you need a ride home later," Cal said.

I faced the patch of dirt, and kneeling down, I began to dig. "I think I'd rather drink a gallon of Emma's tea than do this," I grumbled.

Simon tipped his head back and let forth a belly laugh. I had forgotten about his heightened wolf hearing. *I'm beginning to hate you old man.*

Chapter 35

Cal was as good as his word and drove me home that evening. I was sweaty and covered with dirt, so we skipped our usual cuddle time in the truck. After a shower, and what felt like hours of scrubbing my hands with a nail brush and soap, I threw myself on my bed and groaned. Muscles ached that I didn't even know I had before today. I wasn't sure what today's assignment had to do with communicating with my spirit animal, but I was determined not to let Simon win. If this was another one of his tests, then I would just go along with it for now. I sank blissfully into the covers and drifted off to sleep.

I was on a sun baked plain of dry grasses and dusty soil. *Was I dreaming again?* I looked for Calvin's wolf spirit, turning is a complete circle, but he was nowhere to be seen. The ground suddenly shook and I fell to my knees. As my hands touched the dry dirt, I suddenly felt *connected* to something, or someone, almost as though they were calling out to me. A large shiny carapace then appeared, rising up from a hole in the earth. A huge scarab stood before me moving its arms in a strange motion while spinning something between what I guessed were its hands.

"I am busy little one," the scarab's voice echoed in my head. "Why have you called upon me?"

Had I somehow called my spirit animal by working with the soil in Simon's garden?

"Uh, sorry about that," I said. "I'm not sure how this works yet."

"Yes little one, you are still young," the scarab said, "and have yet to learn the way to walk the world of dreams and darkness. Call for me again when you have learned the way of such things."

The whole time the scarab was speaking its hands never ceased their strange movement and a sphere was growing between them.

"Wait, I think I need your help now," I said. "I don't know how to call on the wolf spirit who is supposed to shield me and I've been told that in a month I'll be attacked by spirits of the dead."

The scarab turned its head to the side. Was it looking at me? It was hard to tell.

"It is true that the spirits of the dead plague those like you once their power has awakened," the scarab's words echoed. "If the night the dead walk your world is nearing, then head my words. Drum a beat to gain your wolf's attention. Focus your thoughts on what you require of him and continue to lead him with your drumming. If the situation is urgent, then drum the beat with your feet as you dance. Lead your wolf to your side, then become the flickering flame that leads the spirits of the dead out of darkness."

The sphere that the scarab had been spinning was now larger than her. I realized suddenly that it was a huge ball of manure. She then bowed to me and turned facing the horizon. The sun had begun to set as we had talked and she started rolling her ball of manure towards the setting sun, her silhouette black against a rose colored sky. *A dung beetle sunset.* I never imaged that such a thing could be so beautiful.

Chapter 36

*A*fter two weekends of training with Simon, three if you count the first weekend at Wolf Camp, he decided that I was ready to attempt communicating with Jackson Green. I had never forgotten about Jackson, his vinegar smell was hard to ignore, but I had promised Cal that I wouldn't reach out to Jackson's ghost until Cal and I were both ready.

Calvin was making progress speaking with his wolf spirit. They didn't really speak yet in words, but they could pass feelings along to one another and occasionally Calvin could focus his intention to make a request.

I was learning how to focus on the location of spirits of the dead, so that I could pinpoint Jackson's location rather than a vague smell impression. I had also learned to reach out to Calvin's wolf spirit. This was really difficult and it didn't help that my concentration was shattered around Cal. It was hard for me to block out Calvin's face, voice, and smell and focus on touching his wolf spirit.

It was also difficult for me to get over my shyness about dancing in front of other people, especially Cal. I would have been fine on a dance floor filled with other dancers, or heck if there had at least been music to dance to. When calling spirit, however, I had learned that I had to provide the beat. I would be calling Calvin's wolf spirit to me and though slapping my hands together would occasionally catch its attention, we had discovered through trial and error that dancing was the most reliable method. My spirit animal had been right. Dancing created a much stronger link to Cal's wolf spirit. *I would just have to learn to get over the embarrassment.*

Calvin and I had finally made progress though and Simon said that we needed to practice against a potential threat. He didn't need to remind us that we had to be ready to face multiple threats very, very soon. Samhain was only a month away. That was something never far from our minds.

I remembered Emma being with us the first time we tried my Ouija board way of communicating with Jackson's ghost. I felt a twinge of regret that she couldn't be with us now. I hoped that we could confide in Emma some time soon. Until then it was just me and Cal...and Simon. Simon was here to watch, though Calvin assured me that if something started to go wrong Simon could provide emergency backup. I was going to be dealing with only one lost soul, so I wasn't worried about whether Simon *could* provide assistance but whether or not he *would*. He had some strange ideas about how to define a learning experience. Hopefully he wouldn't think that letting part of my own spirit essence slip away into the light was just an acceptable way to learn a lesson.

Simon, Cal and I had met at the cabin and moved the few pieces of furniture against one wall, giving us a small, clear area in which to do our thing. Cal and Simon each sat in a corner facing me while I stood in the open space. Though I would begin by stomping out a beat with my foot, it would end up leading into the dance to call Cal's wolf spirit.

I'm still not sure why only Calvin's wolf spirit responds to my call. Cal seems to think it has something to do with our being soul mates. Perhaps it was our feelings for each other that formed a deeper connection on some spiritual level. I may not fully understand how I was able to call his wolf, but I did know that we had been having good results.

It was time to test our training when a ghost was involved. I took a deep breath to clear my mind and then tried to focus on the image of Calvin's wolf. Stomping my left foot against the wood floor I clapped in time to the beat. Once I had the beat set I stopped clapping and raised my arms out wide at shoulder height. In my mind's eye I called out to Calvin's wolf spirit and heard a howl in return.

It was hard not to look over to Cal for confirmation. I knew that he often flinched when a connection was made, but looking at Calvin could make me lose his wolf's attention. It could also make me fall flat on my face. *I am so not going to look at you Calvin Miller.*

Picturing Cal's wolf spirit striding towards me, I began to walk in a clockwise circle. I never stopped stomping my left foot to keep the beat as I circled. I swayed a bit, probably more from dizziness than from any particular dance move, and began to pick up my pace. As the beat increased in cadence I pictured Calvin's wolf switch from an easy lope to a run. Running and running, stomping and stomping until suddenly I felt the hair on my arms and the back of my neck rise. I felt sure that Calvin's wolf was now here with me. It was something I knew without needing confirmation from Cal.

I stopped dancing and sat on the floor facing Calvin and Simon. Reaching to my right I pulled out my makeshift Ouija board and took a steadying breath. *Jackson time.*

"Jackson, do you wish for me to turn our murder evidence over to the police?" I asked.

O.k. calling it evidence was a bit of a stretch. We really just had some wild theories, copies of newspaper articles from the library and Internet, a box full of legal documents, and pictures of what we assumed was a poisonous plant growing in Grace Green's herb garden. It wasn't enough to convict someone of murder, not by a long shot, but it did have the potential to open an investigation. Was that something Jackson would want? *I was about to find out.*

Holding my hand over my notepad I pointed at YES. Nothing. No vinegar smell or dizziness. I waited a moment then moved my finger to point at MAYBE. Again nothing. Bracing myself for what was to come next I moved my hand to point at NO. The sensation was overwhelming. I felt as though I was drowning in a sea of noxious vinegar and couldn't tell which direction was up. Working as I had trained with Simon, I fought to call up an image of Cal's wolf spirit and my intention. *Help me.* The vertigo was gone as fast as it had begun and the vinegar smell had faded. *Thank you.*

"So that's a definite no on sending evidence to the police," I said trying to sound calm. "O.k. Jackson next question," I said. "Do you wish for me to send your box of cash and legal documents to your wife, Grace?" I asked.

I was expecting a big no on this one. Jackson may not want to drag his wife into a murder investigation, but I couldn't imagine him wanting her to profit from his murder. I held my hand out to point at the word YES. My head was flooded with vinegar smell and dizziness. *Son of a dung beetle.* Jackson had forgiven his wife after all. I called on Cal's wolf spirit faster this time, banishing the smell impression and dizziness.

Shifting my focus, I looked at Simon and Calvin who sat across from me on the floor. "Any other questions for Jackson?" I asked.

Calvin shrugged and shook his head in the negative while Simon just stared at me. No help from that department. *Figures.* I placed my makeshift Ouija board outside of my invisible circle and pushed myself to my feet. I began stomping out a beat again, stomp stomp, stomp stomp, and moved widdershins, or counter clockwise. I danced and pictured Calvin's wolf spirit loping home. When I could no longer feel his presence I stopped moving and faced Simon and Cal.

"Not bad kitten," Simon said with a wink.

Kitten? With the energy unraveling from me I was too tired for a fight. *You just wait old man.*

116

Chapter 37

The following two days were a blur of action, followed by an agony of waiting. I had called Emma to tell her that Cal and I had done an impromptu séance with Jackson Green and that we were going to be sending his papers to his wife Grace. Emma still wanted Grace to fry, but settled on writing a scathing article about the Green farm's treatment of bees for the school paper. Calvin and I had rushed to follow Jackson's wishes and then we had to sit back and wait for the results.

The first day Emma and I had tried giving each other beauty treatments to kill time and take our minds off the waiting. By the next day I had chewed nearly all the black polish off my fingers and looked longingly at my cup full of pens. I wasn't quite *that* desperate yet. On the third day I woke up to an amazing thing. *Fresh, clean, vinegar free air.*

The lost spirit of Jackson Green was gone. I phoned Calvin who agreed to pick me up early for waffles with ice cream at the nearby diner. Celebrating my non-haunted status by eating waffles dripping with vanilla ice cream had to rank as one of my best moments of all time. It didn't hurt that Calvin was sitting across from me wearing his toothy grin. After mopping up every last bit of breakfast, I sighed. I was in post waffle bliss. Calvin laughed and I sighed again.

"O.k. Yuki, time to go to school," Cal said.

So much for bliss.

When we arrived in the school parking lot I noticed an enormous banner hanging over the school entrance. I looked up at the banner and laughed. In huge red letters someone had painted the words Spirit Week. I laughed so hard that tears rolled down my face and I had to hold my stomach. *Spirit Week?* For the first time in over a month I wasn't being haunted by a spirit and they were having Spirit Week at school? I laughed again. The irony was just too much. It was then that I noticed all of the students entering the building wearing red. I looked over at Cal whose broad chest was covered in a dark red t-shirt. *What was I missing?*

I had been so preoccupied by spirit training and trying to help Jackson's ghost finally find peace that I hadn't noticed that this was the week of homecoming. Spirit Week was a week of school events where students showed their school pride, such as by wearing school colors, followed by the big game and culminating in the homecoming dance. I was stunned by a thought. *Where had September gone?* Then my face burst with a huge smile. *I get to wear my corset dress.* This was going to be the best week *ever*.

Chapter 38

I was still basking in the non vinegar smelling air when I floated into the cafeteria later that day. Over at our table Emma waved me over.

"I knew you wouldn't wear red," Emma said smugly. She was wearing her usual gray and cream.

"Would you believe I didn't even know it was Spirit Week?" I asked.

Emma laughed. "No way, you're just a nonconformist," Emma said, "like me."

I had to agree with her.

"I have good news," I announced, "No more Mr. Smelly."

Emma gaped at me. "Really? Is that why you and Cal needed smootchy time this morning?" she asked.

I had texted her that morning to let her know I didn't need a ride to school. Leave it to Emma to jump to conclusions.

"We weren't smootching. We were eating," I said. *Well we were eating and kissing.*

Looking around the room, Emma turned back to me and said, "I have something to tell you too, but I'm not sure how you'll take it."

I looked back at her wondering what could be so important.

"Yuki, I've been wanting to tell you, but it was never a good time," Emma said while twirling her carrot stick.

I was trying to pay attention, but I had just noticed Cal wading through a sea of students near the lunch counter. He looked so good it was hard for me to concentrate on Emma's words.

"The good news is that I don't think it will bother you all that much anymore," Emma said, getting my attention. "I heard that Garrett has a date for the homecoming dance."

I waited to see if I felt upset. *Nope, no lingering pangs of regret.*

Cal looked back and winked at me as he piled his tray with burgers. I blushed and smiled from ear to ear.

"That's cool. Who's he going with?" I asked.

I didn't really care now who Garrett went to the dance with. Why should I care when I was going to the dance with Calvin?

"Get this," Emma said smugly, "he's going with a cheerleader!" She looked totally scandalized.

"Poser," I gloated.

"Total poser," Emma laughed.

Then I caught a whiff of wet dog smell and Calvin sat down beside me so close our legs were touching.

"Hey Dung Beetle Princess, what's so funny?" Cal asked.

His question only made us laugh harder.

"Sacred Scarab," I corrected him through tears of laughter.

"Sacred Scarab," Calvin said lovingly as he wiped a tear from my cheek. "My sacred scarab."

This really was the best day ever.

Chapter 39

𝓕riday night couldn't come soon enough. The school was buzzing with excitement for the big game and the homecoming dance. I really couldn't care less about the game, but I had been dreaming about the dance for weeks. The full moon was also fast approaching, but Calvin reassured me that we were going to the dance. He had been training with Simon every day after school and was making progress with self control and communicating with his wolf spirit. Cal had promised to pick me up early. I was running late.

I heard my mom let Calvin inside as I finished lacing up my boots. I surveyed my appearance in the bathroom mirror and smiled. *Looking good Yuki.* I was wearing my black strapless corset dress that laced up the back and then flared out in layers of tulle and strategically torn lace. The dress ended above the knee and my boots came just under. That left about two inches of red lace leggings to show my school spirit. I twirled, making the skirt layers float out around me. I felt like a princess, and not the dung beetle kind.

Grabbing my bag, I headed for the stairs. I started hopping down them nearly two at a time until I saw Cal. He had a stunned look on his face and my mom turned to see what he was looking at.

"Honey, you look beautiful," my mom said as I twirled one more time at the bottom of the stairs.

"Thanks," I said.

"Ready?" Calvin asked.

He looked gorgeous. In the dim lighting Cal looked even more tan than usual. He was all in black which made his blue eyes positively glow.

"Absolutely," I answered.

"Have fun you two," my mom said as we made our way out the door.

Oh, I planned to.

When we arrived at the school parking lot, the gymnasium entrance and the trees by the walkway were lit up with tiny white string lights. Cal and I took our time before going inside. The night felt magical and in a good way. We had both been through so much lately. It felt wonderful to have a moment to just enjoy each other's company. Well and there was kissing. *Lots and lots of kissing.*

Eventually we made our way inside. The dance committee had outdone themselves with decorations and the room was filled with red paper flowers. A DJ was playing something slow and there were already couples out on the dance floor. As the song ended couples started to disperse and I was surprised to see Gordy and Emma walking towards us. Together. Calvin raised an eyebrow at me in question, but I was just as surprised as he was.

"I have no idea," I said to Cal, "I didn't even know that Emma was coming tonight."

Emma had avoided my questions about the dance and, being a good friend, I decided not to press her, since I didn't want it to seem like I was rubbing it in that I had a date. *Apparently she has one too.*

Standing in front of Emma and Gordy was like looking into a mirror that reflected back the opposite of Cal and myself. Cal towered over me, while Gordy was at least a head shorter than Emma. I was dressed all in black yet Emma looked elegant in a simple white sheath dress. Even Calvin's and Gordy's suits were totally different. Cal was dressed in an all black, modern cut suit, while Gordy was sporting a light gray suit with a butterfly collar turned up at the neck. It would have looked ridiculous on anyone else, but on Gordy it had a cool geek retro look. Knowing Emma, they had probably bought their outfits at one of the local thrift shops. It would be just like her to make sure even their clothing was recycled.

"Hey," I said looking back and forth between Emma and Gordy. O.k. it sounded lame, even to me, but in my defense I was still in shock.

"Hey Yuki-sama," Gordy said in reply.

Gordy was smiling and Emma was doing her best to look aloof but I saw a wicked gleam in her eye.

"Emma, out with it," I said going for the direct approach.

I couldn't believe she hadn't told me about Gordy. He was *my* friend. I couldn't even imagine how the two of them had met. They didn't have anything in common. *Except me.*

"What's to tell?" Emma said slyly.

I knew that I hadn't been totally forthcoming with Emma lately, but that had been for a good reason. I couldn't share someone else's secret with her. It was up to Calvin to tell Emma about his wolf spirit, but I had known all week that she had felt slighted. She could read me too well and knew I had been holding something back.

"Uh, I didn't realize you two knew each other," I added lamely. *Out with it Emma.*

"Emma stopped by Anime Club the other day," Gordy said, "to let me know you weren't going to make it. She, uh, stayed to watch a movie."

Oh crap. I had forgotten about anime club so hadn't stopped by the media room to let Gordy know I wasn't coming. It had been a really busy week and I had been spending every vinegar free moment with Cal. When I thought about it, I realized that I hadn't been a very good friend to Gordy or Emma this week. The two of them must have been feeling lonely and somehow hooked up. *They don't look lonely now.* Gordy had his arm around

Emma's waist as we talked and he blushed every time I looked at him.

"We had so much fun, I decided to ask Gordy to the dance," Emma added. Emma seemed pleased with herself and I had to admit that the two of them looked great together.

Cal squeezed my hand and asked, "Anyone want something to drink?" He met with a round of "no's" but Gordy offered to go with Cal to the beverage table.

Turning her gleeful look on me, Emma asked, "Want to dance?"

Emma obviously wasn't going to say anything more about her and Gordy tonight. I realized that I needed to burn off some nervous energy and stepped out onto the dance floor with Emma. *I would just have to wait until later to get the details.*

Chapter 40

The DJ had switched to something industrial with a heavy beat that vibrated up through the soles of my boots and resonated with the beating of my heart. Yes, after the worry and constant training of the last month, I was ready to let loose. I started stomping my feet and dancing to the music. I raised my arms above my head and thought of how I was finally free of being haunted. *I was free.* We had done something special by helping Jackson's spirit find peace and I was feeling happy. I was also here at the dance with a super hot date and surrounded by my friends. I was soaring high and the tempo of the music picked up. The beats were coming faster and I was dancing with all my energy. *I was free.*

I was vaguely aware of Emma dancing nearby and of someone calling my name. *Yuki.* It wasn't Emma's voice though. *No, it was Cal.* There was something about his voice. He sounded worried, distraught, but I didn't want to open my eyes. I didn't want to stop dancing. I was happy here. *I was free.*

That was when I saw it. In my mind's eye I saw Calvin's wolf spirit rushing towards me. No, it was rushing towards Cal. *Oh God, what had I done?* I forced my eyes open, but was having trouble breaking free of the dance. Calvin was staring at me from across the room, stricken with fear. *Yuki.* He tried yelling my name one more time and in terror I watched as his hair lengthened and something feral slipped behind his eyes. *No, no, no this can't be happening.*

We shouldn't have come tonight. It was too close to the full moon. We were still learning to control our powers.

How could we have risked everything for a stupid school dance? *How could I have done this to Cal?*

Trying to focus my will, I forced out an order for the wolf spirit to leave us. It didn't work. Cal's wolf was too strong this close to the full moon. Knowing that the energies I had built up from the dance were not going to help us, I tore myself from the dance floor. I grabbed Emma's arm as I went. She must have seen the fear in my eyes because she didn't demand to know why I was dragging her across the room. I searched the crowd for Calvin's face, hoping he could hold the transformation at bay. *Just a little longer Cal. I'm coming.*

We found Calvin leaning against the wall near where I had last seen him. He was sweating and breathing hard, but he hadn't fully changed yet. With the dim lighting and huge crowd no one had probably noticed anything strange, but we needed to get Cal out of here fast.

"Emma, we need to get Calvin outside now!" I yelled over the music.

I must have looked really freaked because Emma didn't balk at my ordering her around. She got under one of Calvin's arms and I got under the other. He was a big guy but we managed to get him to a side door. This door led to a hallway that ran behind the gym with dark openings leading to the locker rooms. We followed the hall to the end, where a glass door would take us outside.

"Emma, I know this is not the best time to tell you this, but Calvin is a werewolf," I huffed as we dragged Cal further down the hall.

Calvin was trying to help us by putting one foot in front of the other, but his dress shoes were starting to drag more with each step. To her credit Emma didn't flip out.

"I knew you two were hiding something," Emma said simply.

Leave it to Emma to take this in stride. This was one of those times I felt lucky to have her as a friend.

126

Once we were outside, I asked Emma to go get her car. She pulled off her high heeled shoes and ran for the parking lot. I was sprawled on the ground with Calvin, praying that we could make it in time. We needed to get out of here before any school security or chaperones from the dance noticed us. Plus, I didn't want to think about what could happen if Cal fully transformed while feeling trapped here amongst the entire student body. I shivered, though not from the night chill.

"Hang in there Cal," I said holding him in my lap, "just a little longer. Hold on just a while longer."

I was rocking back and forth and had tears streaming down my face. Anyone wandering around the side of the gymnasium would have thought I had completely lost my mind.

Cal clung to me and whimpered as Emma pulled her car up to the curb. With her help I was able to get Calvin into the back seat.

"We need to drive to that cabin behind Calvin's house," I said to Emma, "the one that his dad uses as a workshop."

I was hoping that Simon would be there, but even if the cabin was empty it would be a safer place for Cal to change than here.

"We need to get him away from other people," I added.

Emma glanced at me once in the rear view mirror and with a nod she drove off. Driving through town she was careful not to exceed the speed limit, but she stepped on the gas when we made it to the back roads. We were going so fast that we nearly didn't make the turn onto the dirt road to the cabin. With a huge thud she drove over a boulder, but kept driving as we approached the workshop. Light was shining through the curtained windows and I let out a cry of my own. *Please old man, please be here.*

Chapter 41

The cabin was in sight as Emma drove us over the last stretch of bumpy dirt road. We were so close that I could see the lights shining from within the cabin. *Almost there*. It was then that I heard it. There was a whimper and a tearing sound from the back seat and the hand that I was holding pulled away, but not before it had begun to change. I had felt the fur and claws of his hand. *Not his hand his paw.*

"Emma drive faster!" I shouted, "Calvin's changing."

I didn't know what to do. There didn't seem to be enough room in the back seat for a full sized wolf and the rear of the car was filling with a writhing mass of silver fur. My seat was thrust forward as a rear leg slammed into it. I cracked my head on the dashboard but I didn't care. It couldn't be nearly as bad as what Calvin was going through. We came to a sliding stop in front of the workshop and Emma and I ran to open the back doors of the car. Calvin, or rather his wolf since he was now fully changed, immediately tried to leap from the car but one of his front legs caught in a seatbelt. As the wolf lunged out the door there was a sickening snap and he fell forward whimpering.

"Emma," I shouted, "Go get Simon!"

I could only hope that Simon was inside. Emma and Simon hadn't met but we had told her that Calvin had an Uncle Simon who was staying here. Emma ran to the cabin, but the door burst open before she reached it.

"What happened?" Simon demanded, "Where's Calvin?"

"He changed in the car," I said starting to cry again, "His leg..."

I couldn't finish. The sound of Cal's leg snapping echoed through my head. Simon ran to the car and to Calvin. Emma was right behind him and began relaying facts. I had no idea how she stayed so calm.

"It's his right foreleg," Emma said, "The belt was caught around it when he went to jump from the car. Judging from the snap we heard, I believe his leg to be broken."

Broken? I was going to be sick.

"Is his body chemistry that of a wolf now?" Emma asked.

To my surprise, Simon answered her. "Yes," Simon said, "he is fully changed, so for the moment he's wolf."

Emma went around the other side of the car and opened her trunk. She was rummaging around inside as she said, "We need to sedate him. If he continues to struggle against that seat belt he's going to do more damage. I have some herbal tinctures that should be safe."

Emma had been into natural medicine for years and always kept an arsenal of teas, herbs, salves, and tinctures on hand, but I wasn't overly confident about treating Calvin in his wolf form. How would she know what a safe dosage was? In answer to my thoughts, Emma pulled out a toolbox filled with herbal medicines and a large book that she started flipping through.

"How much does he weigh?" Emma asked.

I looked to Simon hoping that he would know.

"Roughly two hundred pounds," Simon said running his hands nervously through his hair.

That was one huge wolf. Emma consulted her book, which at closer inspection appeared to be a reference guide for alternative veterinary medicine. Grabbing a few of the bottles, she put a few drops of dark liquid into a bowl that looked suspiciously like a dog dish.

"Here," Emma said handing the dish to Simon, "make him drink this. It will calm him down."

How was Simon going to get a wolf to drink one of Emma's nasty tonics? I was wringing my hands and praying that Cal would be alright. To my surprise Simon handed the dish to me.

"I'm going to try to hold him, but you'll need to be ready," Simon said grimly.

As we approached, Calvin started growling and trying to run away but he was still caught in the seat belt. Simon stared him down and Calvin slowed his thrashing, but he still showed his teeth.

"Yuki," Simon said, "on three. One, two...three!"

Simon had thrown himself on Calvin and the wolf was snapping and trying to get away. I ran in, hoping Simon knew what he was doing. Simon managed to grab Calvin's muzzle and I poured the liquid into his mouth. O.k. a lot of it ended up on his face, but some of the liquid made it into his mouth. I jumped back but Simon continued trying to hold him still. When I looked into Simon's eyes I could see his wolf looking back at me. Simon was tapping into his wolf's strength to restrain Calvin.

Emma came up beside me and put her arm around my shoulders.

"How long do we have to wait?" I asked her.

"Probably five minutes," Emma said, "I think his body will metabolize it quickly, but I can't be sure. I still have a lot to learn."

It was then I could tell she was shaking. Emma had stayed calm when I had told her Cal was a werewolf and she had driven here while keeping a cool head. She had even made quick decisions about how to sedate him, but now that all we could do was wait she was starting to go into shock.

"How did you know what herbs to use on a wolf?" I asked hoping to distract her.

131

"I didn't really," Emma replied, "but I had a book that I had been studying, so I just looked it up. I was lucky that most of the treatment is similar to what my mom takes for anxiety. I had tons of that tincture in the trunk." Her shaking was subsiding but she still looked a bit wide eyed.

"Do you know how to fix a broken leg?" Simon asked. He was out of breath, but I noticed that Cal was struggling less.

"Fix a wolf's leg?" Emma asked incredulously.

"Does he look human to you?" Simon asked sarcastically.

Simon's arms were covered in blood, most of it his, but Emma wasn't looking at him. Her eyes were focused on Cal.

"Would it be like setting a dog's leg?" Emma asked.

"Close enough," Simon said. "We can't bring him to a hospital and if we brought him to a veterinary clinic he could change right on the table."

"I've seen it done," Emma said slowly, "and I have a few reference books here. I was thinking about studying alternative veterinary medicine, but I didn't know if I could stomach it so I started volunteering at the local shelter."

"Get studying love," Simon.

Calvin was falling asleep in his arms.

Chapter 42

I was rummaging around the cabin for the supplies Emma had asked for. I found ice that Simon was using to keep his beer cold in a plastic cooler and some masking tape on a shelf. I ran back out to the car wishing I hadn't worn a corset dress to the dance. I couldn't take a deep breath and it was adding to my feeling of panic.

Emma had found an old wire coat hanger that she kept in her trunk. She said you never knew when you might need such a thing. *I guess she was right.* Emma also pulled out a roll of gauze and an herbal salve that she said would help with the pain. I handed Simon one of his t-shirts filled with ice, my impromptu ice pack, which he placed on Cal's injured leg. Emma said it was important to reduce the swelling. We had already cut the seat belt free from around Calvin's leg and looked for other injuries. The leg was definitely broken and there were lacerations from his struggle in the car, but otherwise Calvin was fine. *Well, unless you count the part about him being a wolf.*

Emma had me fold the wire hangar several times, approximately the same length as his injured leg. Once the swelling was down Emma slathered a layer of the salve directly on Calvin's leg then began wrapping it in gauze. She wound the gauze around the wire hangar making a splint with the leg in a neutral position. Emma continued wrapping the gauze around Cal's leg and around the splint holding it in place. After the leg had been bound she secured it with tape, being careful to tape the gauze and avoid any adhesive touching his fur. She did this all carefully while Simon continued to hold Cal and I stroked Calvin's neck and head. *I'm so sorry.*

"That's the best I can do," Emma said, "We should try to get him to drink a bit more of the calmative and then move him somewhere safe."

Simon looked exhausted, and bloodied, but he nodded. "We can bring him inside the cabin," Simon said, "he'll be safe enough here. Someone will need to be with him when he changes back. That wrapping is good for a narrow wolf's leg but I'm guessing it won't feel too comfortable on a man's arm."

Oh crap. I hadn't thought of that. What if we had left him and the wrappings had cut into his arm?

"I'll stay," I said. "We can take turns watching him."

I imagined Calvin's arm changing back to its human shape and the tattoo of a wolf chasing a scarab across his bicep. Seeing Cal's tattoo usually filled me warmth, a physical reminder of the bond we shared, but at the moment the image was making me feel sick. I was supposed to be Calvin's anchor to the human world. I was supposed to help ground him here, not call his wolf spirit when he was defenseless. *This was all my fault.*

"No Yuki, as much as the prospect of you spending the night is tempting, you girls need to run home before your parents come looking for you," Simon said.

I wanted to argue with Simon, but I realized that he was right. "I'll be back then in the morning," I said.

"I'll hold you to it Kitten," Simon said playfully.

Emma looked uncomfortable. "Make sure to keep icing that leg," Emma said, "and keep him off it. If he wakes up again before he changes back, then give him two drops of this tincture. Once he's in human form you can give him these herbs. Steep the herbs in one quart of water and give him a cup every two hours for pain." Emma handed Simon a tincture bottle and a packet of herbs.

Knowing we had to go I gave Calvin a hug, careful not to touch his injured leg, and turned to leave. I started crying again as I stepped into Emma's car. I prayed that Calvin would make it through the night.

Chapter 43

*A*t some point during the night's chaos Emma had thought to text Gordy and let him know we were alright. I had forgotten all about Emma's date, and my friend, in the rush to save Cal. Emma texted Gordy that Cal had gotten sick at the dance and that the two of us had helped him to her car to take him home. Emma had gone on to tell him that we tripped while lifting him out of the car and that Cal had fractured his arm. Gordy had wanted to rush off to help us, but Emma had fibbed that we were with his parents and uncle and that as soon as Calvin was settled we'd be heading home for the night. Making sure Gordy could catch a ride with one of the other students at the dance, Emma had promised to talk to him more the next day.

As she told me all this, I wondered again at Emma's clear mindedness. Where was the bookish girl who cried whenever we found a dead bird or squirrel as kids? I had always been the tough one, but suddenly Emma was this calm cool combat medic and I was a gibbering mess. When did things change so drastically?

Emma, still thinking more clearly than me, suggested we stop at an all night convenience store and use their bathroom to freshen up before taking me home. I'm surprised the clerk didn't call the police. Maybe he thought we were practicing for Halloween. We were still in our formal dresses which were covered in dirt and blood. I had twigs and leaves in my hair which was sticking out in every direction. My mascara had run in rivers down my face and my eyes were swollen from crying. But at least I was wearing black. Emma's white dress was ruined. She was covered in blood, dirt, and dribbled medicine that left red and brown blotches all over her dress. What were those patterns called in psychology class? Rorschach ink blotches? I wondered what someone could tell about my current state of mind if they knew what I saw in them.

After we left the convenience store, Emma drove me home. I had so much to say to her, but I couldn't form words. I just cried quietly in the passenger seat.

Pulling into my driveway Emma turned to face me. "He'll be alright Yuki. We have to believe that." Then she was gone.

Somehow I made it up to my room and changed out of the soiled dress. I held one of the beetle plushies that Cal had given me and prayed for him to make it safely through the night. I would visit him first thing in the morning. *But would he want to see me?* I fell to sleep thinking about love, pain, and regret and hoping against hope for forgiveness.

Chapter 44

I walked to the workshop, deep in thought. As I approached the cabin I was surprised to see Cal's dad come through the front door. He waved me over and I quickened my pace.

"Yuki, I'm glad you're here," he said, "Calvin is sleeping, but he's doing fine. His arm is broken, but Simon was able to rewrap the splint you kids made."

So he must have changed back. I nearly fainted with relief. I had been so worried that something would go wrong with the change in his injured state or that he wouldn't be able to shift back at all.

"What you three did was very brave," Cal's dad said. "Thank you."

I didn't think I could handle Cal's dad thanking me right now. I had put his son in danger and risked having their secret revealed. My irresponsible actions had caused this and it was likely that I had lost my friend in the process. When Cal wakes up he wasn't going to want his dad thanking me, he was probably going to hate me forever.

"Don't thank me," I said. "It was my fault." *My fault, my fault, my fault.*

"Yuki, don't be so hard on yourself," Cal's dad said looking concerned.

I couldn't quite meet his gaze. His eyes looked so much like Calvin's that I ached to turn back time so that I could see love in Cal's eyes again.

"When you have time could you have your friend Emma call me?" he asked. "I'm not sure how serious she is about studying medicine, but if she's willing I have a proposition for her. I've made some calls and many of us have agreed to help with tuition if she chooses to study locally. There's a good veterinary medicine program a few hours away at Tufts University."

His words weren't quite sinking in. Did they want Emma to study to be a vet? *Why?*

In answer to my unspoken question he said, "We could use someone who can help us in our wolf form when emergencies come up and not many know about our condition. If Emma's interested have her call me."

Then he was gone.

With no more reason to delay I walked towards the cabin.

As I lifted my hand to knock, Simon opened the door. He looked tired, with dark circles ringing his eyes, but he greeted me with his scar tilted smile. "Why hello Kitten," Simon said slyly, "you're here bright and early. Couldn't stay away from my irresistible charm?"

He opened the door wider as he said the last and I pushed my way inside. I had to see Calvin. I needed to see with my own eyes that he was alright. Against the far wall was a cot piled high with blankets. Walking closer I could see Cal's head asleep on the pillow and his injured arm propped on a cushion beside him.

"He's alright love," Simon said moving to the hotplate beside the old kiln. "Let's make him some of that tea for when he wakes up."

Tea? Oh yah, the herbal stuff Emma handed Simon last night.

"You'll want sugar for that," I said automatically.

Emma's teas were often bitter. *More like disgusting.* If it could help ease Calvin's pain though, I would make sure he drank the entire cup.

I stepped away from the cot letting Calvin sleep.

"You want to tell me what happened?" Simon asked.

Oh god, I had been dreading this. Last night I had told Simon it was my fault but I hadn't been specific. How could I tell him that I had nearly killed Calvin and put

140

them all in danger because I was *dancing*? To my surprise the words flew from my mouth.

"We went to the school dance and I was stupid," I said, "I was feeling so happy about being there and about not being haunted anymore. I went on the dance floor with Emma and we danced. I felt so free." I was shaking so hard I had to set the mug down that I had picked up from the counter. "I didn't know what would happen," I added.

There. It felt better to tell someone.

"If I had known," I said, "then I never would have done it."

I looked up at Simon to see a momentary flash of panic and then it was gone replaced by his usual flirtatious grin.

"In that case Love," Simon said, "the fault is all mine."

What?

He wasn't making any sense. Simon hadn't even been there. How could this be his fault?

"I was teaching you both about control," he said, "and I taught you how to call Calvin's wolf spirit, but I never warned you against dancing for fun. How could you have known what would happen? I should have realized and warned you, but I didn't. It's not your fault Yuki, it's mine."

I felt relief wash through me and then guilt for letting Simon take the blame.

"Well then, we're both at fault," I said.

I looked over at the cot and hoped that Cal would be as understanding. He was alive but I still might lose him. *Please don't hate me Calvin Miller.*

Chapter 45

Simon had left to buy groceries and I sat holding Calvin's hand while watching the red and gold leaves fall outside the cabin window. Autumn had ever been my favorite time of year and the trees bursting with color had always seemed so beautiful. Today the leaves reminded me of all my bright hopes and dreams falling to the earth to shrivel and die and be covered in snow. *Yuki*. I looked back to Cal's hand. Had he just squeezed my hand or did I imagine it?

"Yuki," Calvin croaked.

His eyes slowly fluttered open and I was surprised that they didn't immediately fill with hatred. *It's my fault, it's my fault, it's my fault.*

"Yuki?" Cal asked looking worried.

He probably couldn't remember much from the night before. I was going to have to fill him in on what he had missed. *On how I had ruined things.*

"I'm here," I said. "You should rest. Your arm is broken."

Remembering the tea I began to stand. Calvin held on to my hand more tightly.

"Don't go," he said, "we need to talk."

This was it. He was going to break up with me. It was over. A tear slipped past my defenses and ran down my cheek.

"I'm sorry," I said, "I'm so sorry." I started to cry.

"Yuki," Cal said squeezing my hand. "It's o.k. I remember what happened and it wasn't your fault."

Had he hit his head? Of course it was my fault.

143

"I was stupid," I said. "I never should have stepped foot on that dance floor. I was being selfish and you paid the price." A price that could have been so much higher.

"Yuki, you were just having fun," Calvin said incredulously, "which is what we were there for. You didn't know that dancing would call my wolf spirit to the surface."

Was he forgiving me? If so, I was the luckiest girl in the world.

"If anyone is to blame it's me," Calvin said firmly. He looked away for a moment but when he looked back his eyes were earnest. "Yuki, the dance was too close to the full moon," Calvin said, "but I was stubborn. I thought I could control the change. I wanted to go to the dance with you so badly that I ignored the risk."

Why was everyone blaming themselves? Could it be true that none of us were solely to blame for what happened?

"So you're not mad at me?" I asked, wiping tears from my face.

"Yuki, I'm not mad at you," Cal said trying to sit up. "I love you."

Then he reached out and pulled me to him. We sat there holding each other and alternating between laughter and tears. I had been so worried, but Calvin still loved me. We were going to be o.k.

"Uh Yuki," Cal said, "I think I'm going to be sick."

I pulled away to see that Calvin had gone deathly pale and his face was covered in sweat. *Oh crap.* So much for our romantic moment.

I helped Calvin lay back on the pillows and placed a cool cloth on his forehead. I set a large pottery bowl beside the bed. *Just in case.*

"Emma left us herbs for tea," I said grabbing the mug and handing it to him. "She said it would help with the pain."

He was obviously in tremendous pain and hugging me with a broken arm hadn't helped the situation. Sipping

144

the foul smelling tea he grimaced. "Oh god, this stuff is horrible," Calvin moaned. "I didn't think I could feel any worse." Taking a deep breath he drank a bit more. "I was wrong," Cal said, "this is much worse."

He probably wasn't kidding. I had been Emma's victim more than once and her remedies came with a price.

"More sugar?" I asked.

"Please," Calvin said and laughed.

Even ashen, slick with sweat, and lined with pain, his face smiling at me was the most beautiful thing I had ever seen. *I love you so much Calvin Miller.*

Chapter 46

*A*n hour after drinking Emma's tea, Calvin was feeling better. Color had returned to his face and he seemed to be in less pain. We had been talking about the dance, before things had turned crazy, and were laughing.

"I was really surprised when Emma showed up with Gordy," Calvin was saying, "but they looked good together."

"If we had all stayed at the dance, we probably would have been competing for homecoming King and Queen," I joked.

"You'll always be my dung beetle princess," Cal said lovingly.

How many guys could make a girl weak in the knees calling her *that*? Leaning in I gave him a kiss as keys jingled in the door and it opened to reveal Simon carrying bags of groceries.

"Ah, young love," Simon sighed dramatically, "so pure and innocent...and boring." Simon rolled his eyes at us and headed for the corner that doubled as the cabin's kitchen. "If you ever tire of the cub, I could teach you a thing or two," Simon added slyly.

I could feel my face blushing and Cal suddenly had a lot of color back in his face. Calvin usually let Simon's flirtatious comments slide, but I didn't think he was in the mood for this today.

"Simon, did you buy any more sugar?" I asked trying to change the subject.

"Do you doubt my shopping abilities?" Simon asked holding his hand over his heart. "You have wounded me deeply. Of course I bought sugar, Love. I wouldn't make the poor boy drink that swill without it."

Just then Emma walked through the door. "It's not swill," Emma said. "It's medicine."

Son of a dung beetle. This cabin was too small for a full out Emma and Simon fight so I tried to distract her from Simon who was grumbling that her tea tasted like something he once scraped off his shoe. How he knew what something he scraped off his shoe tasted like, I don't even want to know.

"Emma, come see your patient," I said waving her over to Calvin's bedside.

Emma came over with her arms crossed and looked down at Cal. "You owe me big time Calvin Miller," Emma said.

Calvin suddenly smiled widely. "You're my white knight in shining armor Emma. Thanks."

"No big," Emma said. She shrugged but a smile stretched across her face. "It's good to see you awake and back to your non-furry self," Emma added.

Oh crap.

Emma now knew Calvin's secret and she probably wasn't going to let him forget it. She pulled a packet of herbs from her pocket and held them up in the air. "I expect to see you drink this before I leave," Emma said smugly. "All of it. Otherwise I'll go to the school paper about how our school is infested with werewolves."

Emma was enjoying herself but Simon growled.

"Here," she said tossing the packet to Simon, "brew this up into two cups. You need to drink one too. It will prevent infection in those cuts on your arms."

Simon growled again as he snatched the herbs from the air. "Love, your tea smells worse than dog crap on a hot summer day," Simon said glaring. "I am not going to drink this."

Oh, this was so not good.

Calvin surprised us all by speaking up. "Simon, if I have to drink this then you do too," he said, "and Emma's right, those are some nasty cuts."

Simon was looking beaten when Emma added, "You *would* know what dog crap smells like wouldn't you dog boy." She sniffed and turned away from him.

Simon looked like he was going to kill her, but then grinned. "If you wanted my body Kitten," Simon growled, "all you had to do was ask."

Then the two of them were at it again. I heard something about "playing hard to get" and "over my dead body" as they became louder. Well, I guess the truce was over. Emma and Simon had managed to get along when Cal's health was at risk, but now there was nothing to hold them back. I turned to Calvin and shrugged. Let them fight. I didn't care anymore. Looking into Cal's eyes all I could think of was how much I loved him and how glad I was that he was safe.

"Kiss me," Calvin said throatily and I did.

Chapter 47

I received a message on my phone that night from Emma. Apparently she and Gordy had met up after her job shadowing at the animal shelter. Over tea at the local coffee shop they had come up with a plan. They had both gone home and changed into black clothes and then Emma picked Gordy up for their stealth mission. Without giving anything away about my ability to smell the dead or Calvin's shape shifting, Emma had informed Gordy about Grace Green. I'm not sure exactly what she told him but she must have mentioned that we were all concerned about this older widow who now lived alone on the farm.

Gordy and Emma had proceeded to sneak to the farm and walk quietly up to the house on the hill. Emma snapped some pictures of Grace's herb garden that she then sent to my phone. Where the Deadly Nightshade had grown now stood a beautiful bunch of white flowers. Emma had included a message with the photo. *Yuki, white flowers mean forgiveness.*

I almost expected to smell vinegar as I read Emma's message but the spirit of Jackson Green was no longer trapped here haunting me. I had, with the help of my friends, led Jackson's spirit to the light where his soul could now rest in peace.

I smiled at the picture. I was glad to see that Grace Green was now working towards her own peace. She may have committed a terrible crime but she had also been distraught over the tragic deaths of her three sons. I hoped that she had finally come to forgive her husband and could now begin to forgive herself.

Chapter 48

I visited Calvin frequently over the next few days. It was the weekend so I didn't have to worry about missing school and my parents were used to me spending the weekends with Simon and Cal. Calvin's parents were in the woods north of here, but they called each day to check on how he was healing. I felt sorry for them. The full moon was keeping them away from their home and from their son, but they promised to return home soon. Simon had incredible control over his wolf spirit, which is why he had been chosen as our teacher, so he only had to let his wolf run for a few hours each night. Cal didn't change into a wolf again during the full moon and I wondered if it was because of his injury or because of his alpha status.

Simon didn't want to take any chances though and made sure that Calvin and I were never left alone for long. I think he was still feeling chagrined over the incident at the school dance. We all were. After all that had happened to us, caution seemed the best approach. Having Simon nearby also had the benefit of my learning more about spirit. I questioned him relentlessly and whenever Calvin slept, Simon and I would work on my control over and awareness of spirit. I wasn't being haunted again, yet, but we knew what was coming on Samhain, the night of Halloween, and the events of the last few days only reinforced our resolve to train every day. I had so much to learn and so little time. *Story of my life.*

Emma also visited each day and made sure that Calvin and Simon were healing properly. Emma and Simon always argued but I think she had been genuinely concerned about the lacerations on his arms. The cuts had been red and swollen that first day, but Emma's tonics and teas seemed to be working. I have no idea how she finally got Simon to drink the medicine she brewed, but his health was quickly improving.

Calvin was also feeling better with each day. His arm gave him pain, and he had to be careful not to move it, but he didn't have a fever and his appetite had returned.

During the full moon Cal and Simon ate bloody steaks and burgers by the ton. Watching them made me queasy and Emma never hesitated to show her disgust, but she did admit to me that she had given up on making Calvin a vegan.

"Calvin's a wolf," she said one day, "and wolves eat meat. It's the natural order of things. I don't have to like it, but I can accept it." Emma had said it simply but I knew it was hard for her to admit. "Don't tell Cal though," she added with a wink, "I still want to argue with him at lunch time."

Chapter 49

*E*mma drove me to school on Monday since Calvin wasn't feeling ready to return yet. *Tomorrow*, he had promised. I ached being away from him for an entire school day, but I was glad he wasn't pushing himself. Cal's parents hadn't returned home yet but they had called the school excusing Calvin for the day and giving permission for me to collect his assignments from his teachers, who all voiced concern when I said that Cal had a broken arm. A few even asked if it had happened at the football game and seemed relieved to hear that he wasn't injured on school grounds. No he broke it while trying to escape a car while in wolf form. *If they only knew.*

Getting one of Calvin's assignments had made me a few minutes late to lunch and I was surprised to see Gordy sitting at our table. Gordy and Emma had their heads close together in discussion and for a moment I wasn't sure if I should interrupt. Emma looked up though and waved me over and Gordy got to his feet to leave.

"Hey Gordy, leaving so soon?" I asked. I hoped he wasn't leaving because of me.

"Sorry Yuki-sama," Gordy apologized, "I have to get back to study hall. Tell Calvin I hope his arm heals soon." Turning to Emma he bent down and gave her a long, slow kiss.

Now that is an interesting development.

Emma positively glowed as she watched Gordy saunter out of the lunch room.

"Anything you wish to share?" I asked.

"He's an amazing kisser," Emma said.

Well, that wasn't exactly what I had in mind. "Ugh, too much information," I said and faked a shudder.

"Well he is," Emma said slyly.

"So are you two dating then?" I asked.

I knew Emma had asked Gordy to the dance, but I hadn't heard much since.

"No I just kiss every guy that sits next to me," she said rolling her eyes, "of course we're going out."

I was glad to hear it. Cal and I had been a little worried with the intensity that Emma and Simon fought and we had been wondering if they secretly had a thing for each other. Gordy was a much safer option. *Safer and younger.*

"We should all go on a double date then when Calvin is feeling better," I said. I tried to picture the four of us hanging out as couples. We were all so different. "There's an anime convention coming up soon in New Hampshire," I said teasingly, "we should all go."

I tried to picture Calvin or Emma in costume. Cosplay wasn't mandatory at an anime con but it was the norm.

"I'm in," Emma said surprising me.

"Really?" I asked incredulously. I had suggested the convention as a joke.

"Why not?" Emma asked. "It's something you and Gordy are in to. Plus, there's a rally against animal cruelty coming up at the State House that I expect you all to go to."

I laughed. Leave it to Emma to turn our double date into a negotiation.

"Deal," I said.

Maybe I'd get to see Calvin wearing eye liner after all. *A girl can dream right?*

Chapter 50

*E*mma dropped me off at the cabin after school, but she didn't stay long. Today was the afternoon that the veterinarian visited the animal shelter where she volunteered and she was determined to shadow him throughout his rounds. I wished her luck and silently hoped that the man had patience. Emma was bound to overwhelm him with questions about every move he would make over the next few hours. *Better you than me doctor man.*

After Emma left I rushed into Calvin's arms. I felt like I hadn't seen him for weeks even though we had only been apart for one day. His injured arm was bound in a sling, but we managed to cuddle just fine. *More than fine.* When we finally came up for air I heard Simon chuckle behind me. *How long has he been standing there?*

"Well Kitten, where's my kiss?" Simon asked playfully. *I was so not going there.*

Calvin stood behind me, still holding me with his good arm, as I turned to face Simon. "So what's on the training schedule for today old man?" I asked.

In answer to my question Simon held up a bag of bread. "You want us eat stale bread?" I asked incredulously.

"No thanks Simon, I'm not hungry," Calvin replied jokingly.

"Why, aren't you two a pair of comedians today," Simon said, "and here I had planned a nice trip to the park for you two."

That got our attention. A nice trip to the park? *Not likely.*

"What gives Simon?" I asked, "You want us to leave a bread crumb trail so we can find our way home?"

Calvin laughed low in his throat and Simon just shook his head.

"No Love, I want you two to do a bit of bird watching," Simon said.

Bird watching? I was totally confused and judging by the curious look on Cal's face he was just as stumped.

"Wolves and crows have a special relationship," Simon added, "and often work in tandem. Wolves will often follow crows to find a food source and crows have been known to warn wolves of danger."

Simon handed me the bag of bread and Calvin shrugged. *I guess we were going crow watching.*

The air was tinged with a crisp October chill, so I pulled my black hoodie from my backpack and added it to my many layers. I had on thick leggings and tall forest green boots laced up to the knee so I should be fine so long as we kept moving. Calvin had a bit more trouble and was only able to put one arm through his coat sleeve. I helped him pull the other side of his coat over his injured arm but he was probably going to freeze if we stayed out here for long. The park was fortunately only a mile away from the cabin and we walked quickly holding hands along the way.

Before reaching the park we heard a crow cry out *caw caw* and watched as it settled on a stone post marking a corner of the town cemetery. I shuddered and tried to pretend it was from the cold. Pulling my hood up against the chill breeze I snuck a sideways glance at the crow. I always avoided the cemetery. *Always.* It gave me the creeps and now that I had come into my powers I definitely did not want to walk past those wrought iron gates. *No way crow, I am not stepping foot in that bone yard.*

Calvin looked down at me and asked, "Should we follow it?"

158

The question was innocent enough and I knew that this was part of Simon's training assignment but it was hard to move against my fear.

"Only if it stays outside the cemetery," I said. "I, um, can't go in there." I hoped I didn't sound like too much of a wimp.

Cal squeezed my hand and nodded. "Right, let's see where it leads," he said. "Maybe it will help me find burgers."

I laughed and immediately felt better. "Simon did say crows are known to lead wolves to food," I said going along with the joke.

How could I be scared of a silly graveyard when I was with Cal? With a flutter of wings the crow flew up into the air and crossed the street to land in front of us. *Lead on Crow Dude.*

Chapter 51

*W*e had followed the crow for over an hour when it circled us playfully and flew away.

"I guess that means we're done for the day," I said.

Calvin looked like he was freezing, but he grinned his toothy smile. "Was it just me or did you feel like it was toying with us the whole time?"

He was right. The crow didn't really lead us anywhere, but it seemed to enjoy our company as we followed it around town. Each time we lagged behind it would fly back to us, call out, and then lead on again.

"It was definitely playing with us," I agreed, "but it never did help you find those burgers."

Cal laughed. "That's alright I'm feeling hungry for something else right now."

He pulled me to him and kissed me deeply. We could have stayed like that forever. I didn't feel cold at all.

When I finally made it home, after saying goodbye to Calvin at the cabin, I had to drag myself up the stairs to my bedroom. I was exhausted. I stretched out on my bed and drifted off to sleep.

I was suddenly standing on a barren plain. *Another dream?* The sky was light overhead but it was quickly darkening as a cloud of thousands of moths raced towards me. Flying ahead of the storm front was a lone crow. After circling me the crow landed on a nearby rock. "Caw caw," the crow called. Apparently I couldn't speak crow. I then looked at what the crow had dropped at its feet.

A chrysalis, with something squirming inside, wiggled on the rock. The crow waited to see that my attention was fixed on the cocoon then took wing, flying away from

the dark mass still moving towards me. I dragged my
eyes from the sky and back to the chrysalis just in time to
see a moth burst forth. The moth hovered above the silk
wrappings and flexed its wings tentatively. As I watched
the moth, I was lost in the dancing patterns swirling like
smoke upon its wings.

It looked as though something just beneath the surface
of the wings was pressing outward as the patterns
continued to swirl. Then, with a gasp, I saw a face press
up just before it was pulled back down into the mist
within the moth's wings. *Was that a soul?*

Looking to the sky I saw it blackening with moths
carrying the spirits of the dead. The fluttering of their
wings had become deafening. Then I fell into dark
oblivion as the moths descended around me.

Chapter 52

I woke up, drenched in sweat, fighting with my covers. I struggled to disentangle myself from the sheets and blankets and pull myself fully into the waking world. This dream had been a foretelling. I could feel it in the tingling of my skin and the heaviness in my heart. The dream crow had tried to warn me and the message was clear. *The spirits of the dead were coming.*

I was willing to bet that Simon knew something like this would happen. When he had me create a garden by digging the soil with my bare hands I had dreamt of my spirit animal the Sacred Scarab, or dung beetle, which burrows into the ground. Yesterday he had Calvin and me follow and observe crows which he indicated had a special relationship with wolves in the wild. Crows have a history of warning other animals, especially wolves, of coming danger. Now I had been sent a warning by the crow in my dream, which had flown ahead of the moth horde carrying the lost souls of the dead.

I had been warned before, that the veil between worlds would thin during Samhain, the night of Halloween, and that the spirits of the dead would be drawn to me. *Like moths to a flame.* The message was indeed clear. We needed to prepare for something almost too terrifying to comprehend. I would be facing an onslaught of spirits haunting me in numbers that could risk my sanity or worse.

I was going to need all the help I could get. Calvin had promised that he and his spirit wolf would stand at my side to face the spirits of the dead. Calvin would be my sword and his wolf would be my shield. From what I had witnessed in my dream I now believed that we truly needed to be ready to face a vast army of lost souls. I hoped that Emma could be convinced to help us prepare medical supplies, something I wished with all my heart we would not need, and I would do my best to enlist Simon's help. Simon may be a roguish playboy and a bit wild, but he had proven himself to be handy in an emergency. But what I would be asking for was potentially dangerous. Could I ask that much from my friends?

Cal and I were also going to have to devote ourselves to our training. I still had a great deal to learn. The recent incident at the homecoming dance had proven that. I was going to have to become adept at focusing my mind and controlling spirit. Calvin's spirit wolf would need firm guidance and I would have to learn how to send messages quickly and with clear intention. Did we have enough time to gain the necessary knowledge and skills? I dearly hoped so.

Chapter 53

Calvin pulled his truck into my driveway and I took a deep breath. I was going to have to tell him about my prophetic dream. Taking one more look at myself in the mirror I decided that I had tried my best. I needed to feel confident today. I had too many favors to ask and couldn't risk wimping out. I had laced up my power boots. Some people own a power tie, but I have a pair of power boots. My power boots were bright red and added an extra two inches to my five foot frame. Wearing these boots, my strappy black top, and black fingerless gloves I felt invincible. I added a red beret, slung a messenger back over my shoulder and was ready for action. *Or at least for high school.*

I took the stairs two at a time and burst out the front door slamming face first into Calvin's chest.

"Didn't realize you were that glad to see me," Cal joked. He slid his good arm around my waist and leaned in for a kiss. "Mmm, I know I'm glad to see you," Calvin added with his toothy grin.

The moment was wonderful but didn't last long enough. I had something important to say and delaying wouldn't make this any easier.

"I had one of my dreams last night," I said.

Calvin looked concerned and I pushed on.

"A crow came to warn me about the lost souls that are coming on Samhain," I said, and shuddered. "Cal, there's just so many of them. They were being carried by a huge swarm of moths and there had to be thousands of them." I had planned to remain calm while retelling my dream but the panic of being enveloped by the spirits of the dead

165

left me breathless. "We need to get ready," I said with fear etching my words. "We need to train more with Simon." I was shaking.

"Yuki, it'll be o.k." Calvin said. "Simon will help us and I'll be at your side. I will always be by your side." Calvin's hand was on my shoulder and he was searching my face. "We can do this," he said quietly.

Just like that, the fear fell away. I believed him. It wouldn't be easy, but we could do this. *Together*.

"O.k.," I said smiling. "Let's do this."

I leaned forward and kissed Calvin once more before we walked to his truck. Once inside the truck I heard my phone beep alerting me of a text message. It was from Emma. "Emma says she has an important announcement to make at lunch today," I said to Cal, "and attendance is mandatory." I laughed at the message.

"Any idea what her big news might be?" Calvin asked.

I thought back over the last few days and all of the major things that had been revealed between us. "Nope, I have no idea," I said, "but knowing Emma it will be huge."

Hopefully it would be good news. I could really use some positive news right now.

Pulling into the school parking lot Cal turned to me and put his arm around my shoulders. "Will you be alright today?" he asked. "That was a really disturbing dream you had thrown at you last night."

I realized while sitting there in his arms that I would be just fine. We had a lot to think about, and plan for, but making myself insane with worry wasn't going to help.

"Yah, I'll be fine," I said as his lips came forward to meet mine.

Better than fine.

Chapter 54

I helped carry Calvin's books to his locker, to where we made a slight detour before heading to lunch. His injured arm was still bothering him, but it was healing rapidly. I wasn't sure if his speedy recovery was due to Emma's medicine, a wolf thing, or a Calvin thing. Cal had always been tough and he seemed determined to be at full strength by Samhain. I was lucky to have him by my side. *I will always be by your side.*

Cal and I walked into the cafeteria hand in hand and neither of us was surprised to see Gordy and Emma waiting at our table. I knew that Gordy didn't have the same lunch as us, but there was no way he would miss Emma's big announcement. She *had* said it was mandatory after all.

Emma looked radiant. Her pale skin and long blond hair nearly glowed and she wore a sly satisfied grin. "Ready for the good news?" Emma asked her gaze falling on each of us in turn.

Gordy squeezed her hand and looked at her with pure adoration. That poor guy had fallen *hard*. Calvin nodded as we took our seats.

"I'm dying of suspense," I said putting my power boots up on the chair next to me. "What's the good news?"

Emma pulled an envelope out of her bag. "Well, according to this acceptance letter," Emma said waving it in my face, "I am now a future student of Tufts University."

Son of a dung beetle.

"Ohmygosh," I blurted, "that's awesome!" *Very, very awesome.* "How did you get in so fast?" I asked.

I think the guys were just as curious, but I was beating them to the punch.

"I submitted my application for early admissions the day after homecoming," Emma said.

Homecoming. Emma had helped to save Calvin's arm, and possibly his life, when he was injured in wolf form. Her role in the events of that night had helped her decide to pursue veterinary medicine as a career.

"It helped that I had a fabulous list of references," Emma added.

I'm sure that that list included Calvin's parents. Thinking back to all of the animal rights projects that Emma had been actively involved with over the years, I realized there were probably hundreds of names on that list.

"Hey girl," I said, "I think you're actually overqualified. They should be paying you to go there."

"Truer words have never been said," Calvin added.

I knew how much Calvin appreciated Emma's help in healing his arm and was a major supporter of her interest in becoming a veterinarian.

"Well I can't complain," Emma smiled. "I *am* getting a free ride after all."

Gordy and Calvin cheered.

A free ride. I had forgotten about Cal's dad's offer to come up with Emma's tuition if she agreed to assist the werewolves when they had need of someone with veterinary training.

"It doesn't get any better than that," I said happily.

This meant that we would always have ties to each other. No matter what happens next. Emma, Calvin, and I would always be together.

So long as I survive Samhain.

Don't miss these books by E.J. Stevens:

Spirit Storm (Spirit Guide, #2) releasing 2011

From the Shadows

A collection of dark haunting poetry. Stevens' work rekindles the great lyrical storytelling style of Edgar Allen Poe with a dark imagination influenced by such masters as Neil Gaiman and H. P. Lovecraft.

Praise for E.J. Stevens and From the Shadows:

"E.J. Stevens' From the Shadows is lyrical magic that will bring chills to your spine and a sigh to your soul. Ms.Stevens paints a vividly haunting picture of love, loss, joy, sorrow, and a myriad of emotions in between. This is a collection to be cherished by fans of poetic storytelling, who aren't afraid of the dark!"
--Lisa Phillips, author of Obsession Everlasting

"For anyone that loves dark poetry, I think you'll love this book of poetry written by E.J. Stevens as well....there's depth to these poems, with a story to be told in each one."
--Gracen Miller, Moonlight Lace and Mayhem

"With From the Shadows, poetess EJ Stevens has produced a slim volume thick with dark thoughts and full of finely wrought imagery....It's a collection of pieces full of power and humor, and leaves the reader anxious to follow Stevens back into the shadows for more."
--Andrew Valentine, author of Bitter Things

"My favorite paranormal poet."
--Bonnie Lea Elliott, Soul Circle

"Wonderfully, strangely, darkly beautiful with powerful imagery throughout....the epitome of poetry."
--Shannon Bailey, Bailey's Books

"As soon as I read the first poem, "Shadow Queen of the Sidhe" I was hooked and did not get up until I finished the entire book!"
--Kelli, I'd So Rather Be Reading

Shadows of Myth and Legend

A collection of dark faerie tales, inspired by folklore, myth and legend, told in the haunting lyrical style of dark poet E.J. Stevens.

Praise for E.J. Stevens and Shadows of Myth and Legend:

"The poetry of EJ Stevens is dark, sometimes lyrical and always interesting. Stevens beautifully paints images with words, tells stories within the poems and holds onto a magical quality that is quite stunning.

I just want to sit back and enjoy the flow of the words, the haunting world of myth and legend, of paranormal creatures and beasts of times long gone that Stevens has immortalized in the written word.

And enjoy it I did."
--Roxanne Rhoads, Fang-tastic Books

"filled with poems about vampires, demons and other creatures of the night. It is not your typical book of poetry but "dark poetry". I have always been a fan of the supernatural and I enjoyed the book. The author has a wonderful imagination and some of her poems were chilling. I recommend this book to everyone who is not afraid of the dark and what lurks within it."
--Melissa, Books R Us

"I really enjoyed this little work of Art! I was lulled into the dark mind of a poet, and taken on a trip. It was fantastic, and I had so many favorites, though this stood out to me: Grindylow - Page 45. I love a great horror, and this was one of those tales that did not disappoint me in the scare department!
I recommend this delectably dark book to every one!"
--Freda, Freda's Voice

"The first thing that stands out about this collection of poetry is the amount of talent that E.J. Stevens has. This isn't some slapped together version of poems put into a book for people to enjoy. Instead there is an immense collection of very dark poems. Each poem brings about a picture from some of the creatures of legends and although it doesn't describe every movement of these creatures I could vividly imagine the darkness that trailed behind all these creatures.

Shadows of Myth and Legend is perfect for any fan of dark creatures that are from legends and fairy tales and will make a great collection of poems for the dark poetry lover. Even if one isn't a dark poetry fan it's worth it to see what that style is all about."
--Cindy Hannikman, Fantasy Book Critic

"Now, I want you to think about all the creatures you read about in paranormal books. Now take all those creatures and put it in poetry. That is the basis of this book. The author has beautiful poetry featuring wolves, vampires, fae, gnomes, zombie's, unicorns, sirens, reapers and more. Each poem is wonderfully written and has a dark feel to each one. I really enjoyed each one, and the feel of each one. "
--Amy, My Overstuffed Bookshelf

"EJ Stevens' Shadows of Myth and Legend is a fascinating collection of short, powerful poems that thrill, chill and delight. Delving into established mythology, Stevens brings all manner of mythical creatures out of the shadows for a glimpse of the world behind the curtain."
--Andrew Valentine, author of Bitter Things

About the Author

E.J. Stevens is the author of the haunting collection of dark poetry From the Shadows and of the chilling collection of paranormal poetry Shadows of Myth and Legend.

E.J. is a graduate of the University of Maine at Farmington with a Bachelor of Arts in Psychology. She has worked a variety of jobs that demonstrate the human condition including schools, psychiatric hospitals and (*shudder*) shopping malls. E.J. currently resides in a magical forest on the coast of Maine where she finds daily inspiration for her writing.

Visit E.J. Stevens at:
http://www.FromTheShadows.info

CPSIA information can be obtained at www.ICGtesting.com
Printed in the USA
LVOW081002010412

275636LV00002B/16/P

9 780984 247523

[9]